PAY ATTENTION, CARTER JONES

CHMIDT

PAY ATTENTION, CARTER JONES

CLARION BOOKS
Houghton Mifflin Harcourt
Boston   New York

CLARION BOOKS

3 Park Avenue, New York, New York 10016

Copyright © 2019 by Gary D. Schmidt

All rights reserved. For information about permission to reproduce
selections from this book, write to trade.permissions@hmhco.com or to
Permissions, Houghton Mifflin Harcourt Publishing Company,
3 Park Avenue, 19th Floor, New York, New York 10016.

Clarion Books is an imprint of Houghton Mifflin Harcourt Publishing Company.

hmhco.com

The text was set in Fairfield LT Std.

Library of Congress Cataloging-in-Publication Data
Names: Schmidt, Gary D., author.
Title: Pay attention, Carter Jones / Gary Schmidt.
Description: Boston ; New York : Clarion Books, Houghton Mifflin Harcourt, [2019]
Summary: Sixth-grader Carter must adjust to the unwelcome presence of
a know-it-all butler who is determined to help him become a gentleman,
and also to deal with burdens from the past.
Identifiers: LCCN 2018033909 | ISBN 9780544790858 (hardback)
Subjects: CYAC: Butlers—Fiction. | Family life—Fiction. | Conduct of life—Fiction.
Middle schools—Fiction. | Schools—Fiction. | BISAC: JUVENILE FICTION / Family
/ General (see also headings under Social Issues). | JUVENILE FICTION /
Social Issues / New Experience. | JUVENILE FICTION / Sports & Recreation
/ General. | JUVENILE FICTION / Social Issues / Death & Dying.
Classification: LCC PZ7.S3527 Pay 2019 | DDC [Fic]—dc23
LC record available at https://lccn.loc.gov/2018033909
Printed in the United States of America
DOC 10 9 8 7 6 5 4 3 2 1
4500739491

For Rebecca Lucy,
with your father's love

• 1 •

THE PLAYERS

Cricket teams, both batting and fielding, may have up to eleven players each. The captain of the batting team determines the order of the batsmen; the captain of the fielding team sets players in positions determined by the style and pace of the bowler.

IF IT HADN'T been the first day of school, and if my mother hadn't been crying her eyes out the night before, and if the fuel pump on the Jeep had been doing what a fuel pump on a Jeep is supposed to be doing, and if it hadn't been raining like an Australian tropical thunderstorm—and I've been in one, so I know what it's like—and if the very last quart of one percent milk hadn't gone sour and clumped up, then probably my mother would never have let the Butler into our house.

But that's what the day had been like so far, and it was only 7:15 in the morning.

7:15 in the morning on the first day of school, when the Butler rang our doorbell.

I answered it.

1

I looked at the guy standing on our front stoop.

"Are you kidding?" I said.

That's what you would have said too. He was tall and big around the belly and wearing the kind of suit you'd wear to a funeral—I've been to one of those too, so I know what a funeral suit looks like—and he had a bowler on his head. A bowler! Which nobody has worn since, like, horses and carriages went out of business. And everything—the big belly, the funeral suit, the bowler—everything was completely dry even though it was an Australian tropical thunderstorm outside because he stood underneath an umbrella as big as a satellite disk.

The guy looked down at me. "I assure you, young man, I am never kidding."

I closed the door.

I went to the kitchen. Mom was tying back Emily's hair, which explains why the dry Ace Robotroid Sugar Stars Emily was eating were dribbling out both sides of her mouth. Charlie was still looking for her other yellow sock because she couldn't start fourth grade without it—she couldn't she couldn't she couldn't—and Annie was telling her what a baby she was, and Charlie was saying she was not she was not she was not, and just because Annie was going into fifth grade that didn't make Annie the boss of her. Then Charlie looked at me and said, "Does it?" and I said, "You think I care?"

"Carter," my mom said, "your oatmeal is on the stove and you'll have to mix in your own raisins and there's some walnuts too but no more brown sugar. And, Carter, before you do that, I need you to run down to the deli and—"

"There's a guy out on our front stoop," I said.

"What?"

"There's a guy out on our front stoop."

My mother stopped tying back Emily's hair.

"Is he from the army?" she said.

I shrugged.

"Is he or isn't he?"

"He's not wearing a uniform."

"Are you sure?"

"Pretty sure."

My mother started tying back Emily's hair again. "Tell him it's the first day of school and he should go find someone else to buy whatever he's selling at seven fifteen in the morning."

"Annie can do it."

My mother gave me That Look, so I went back to the front door and opened it. "My mom says it's the first day of school and you should go find someone else to buy whatever you're selling at seven fifteen in the morning."

He shook his umbrella.

"Young Master Jones," he said, "please inform your mother that I would very much like to speak with her."

I closed the door.

I went back to the kitchen.

"Did you tell him to go away?" said my mother. I think this is what she said. She had a bunch of bobby pins in her mouth and she was sticking them around Emily's head and Emily was hollering and spitting out Ace Robotroid Sugar Stars at every poke, so it was hard to understand what my mother was saying.

"He wants to talk to you," I said.

"He's not going to—"

A sudden wail from Charlie, who held up her other yellow sock, which Ned had thrown up on. Ned is our dachshund and dachshunds throw up a lot.

"Carter, go get some milk," said my mother. "Charlie, stop crying. Annie, it doesn't help to make faces at Charlie. Emily, if you move your head again I'm going to bobby-pin your bangs to your eyebrows."

I went back to the front and opened the door.

The guy was still standing on the stoop, but the Australian tropical thunderstorm was starting to get in under the umbrella.

"Listen," I said, "my mom's going crazy in there. I have to go to the deli and get milk so we can eat breakfast. And Charlie's crying because Ned threw up on her other yellow sock, and Annie's being a pain in the glutes, and Emily's bangs are about to get pinned to her eyebrows, and I haven't even packed my backpack yet—and that takes a while, you know—and we have to leave soon since we have to walk to school because the fuel pump on the Jeep isn't working, and we only have one umbrella. So just go away."

The guy leaned down.

"Young Master Jones," he said, "if you were able to sprint between wickets with the speed of your run-on sentences, you would be welcome in any test match in the world. For now, though, go back inside. In your room, gather what is needed for your backpack. When you have completed that task, find your mother and do whatever is necessary to insure that she is no longer"—he paused—"going crazy." He angled the umbrella a little to keep off the Australian tropical thunderstorm. "While you are doing whatever is necessary, I will purchase the milk."

I looked at the guy. He was wet up to his knees now.

"Do you always talk like that?" I said.

"If you are inquiring whether I always speak the Queen's English, the answer is, of course, yes."

"I mean the way you say everything like you want it to smell good."

The guy shook the rain off his umbrella. I sort of think he meant to shake it all over me.

"Young Master Jones—"

"And that: 'Young Master Jones.' No one talks like that."

"Obviously, some do."

"And that: 'Ob—vi—ous—ly.' It takes you a whole minute to say it. 'Ob—vi—ous—ly.'"

The guy leaned down. "I am going to purchase the milk now," he said. "You shall pack your backpack. Do it properly, then attend to your mother."

He turned to go.

5

"Are you trying to convert me or something?" I said.

"Yes," he said, without turning back. "Now, to your appointed tasks."

So I went upstairs and packed the new notebooks and old pens and old pencils and my father's old science calculator in my backpack, and I put the green marble in my front pocket—all this did take a while, you know—and then I went down to the kitchen where my mother was braiding Annie's hair and Charlie was sniffing with her arms crossed and Emily was finishing her dry Ace Robotroid Sugar Stars. My mother said, "Where's the milk?" and then the doorbell rang again.

"I'll get it," I said.

Guess who it was.

His pants were wet most of the way up when he handed me a bag.

"I have procured the milk," he said.

"Obviously," I said. "Is it one percent?"

"Certainly not—and mockery is the lowest form of discourse."

He handed me another bag.

"What's this?" I said.

"The package is for Miss Charlotte," he said. "Tell her we are most fortunate that American delicatessens are, though parsimonious in their selection of food items that have seen the light of the sun, at least eclectic."

"She won't know what *eclectic* means."

"Copious."

"That either."

The guy sighed. "The contents are self-explanatory."

I took the bags and closed the door. I carried the milk to the kitchen and set it on the table. Then I gave Charlie the other bag.

"What's this?" she said.

"How should I know?"

"Because you're handing it to me. That's how you should know."

"It's something electric," I said.

"Something electric?"

"I don't know. It's from the guy standing on our front stoop."

My mother looked up from Annie's braids. "The guy standing on our front stoop? He's still there?"

Charlie opened her bag and took out—I know this is hard to believe—brand-new bright yellow socks. She screamed her happy scream. That's the scream she makes that could stop a planet from spinning.

My mother looked at the bright yellow socks, then at the milk.

"It's not one percent," she said.

"Certainly not," I said.

My mother dropped Annie's braids and headed out of the kitchen.

∘ 2 ∘

THE WICKET

The wicket may refer to the stumps and bails placed at either end of the playing surface or to the playing surface itself.

WE WERE ALL behind my mother when she opened the front door.

The guy was still standing there, underneath his satellite-disk umbrella, which wasn't doing much anymore since the Australian tropical thunderstorm was blowing sideways now.

"Who are you?" said my mother.

He gave a little bow and rain waterfalled off the front of his umbrella, just like in an Australian rainforest. "Mrs. Jones, I am an acquaintance of your father-in-law and husband, having served the first for many years and attended the childhood of the second."

"Is he all right?"

"I assume you speak of the second."

My mother put her hands on her hips. She still had a bobby pin tucked in the corner of her mouth, and she put on That Look, so she came off pretty tough.

"Captain Jones was, during our last connection, well enough. I called him ten days ago by telephone to inform him that his father, Mr. Seymour Jones, had passed away."

"Passed away?" said Emily.

The guy leaned down. "I am so very sorry to tell you, Miss Emily, that your grandfather has died."

"She never knew him," said my mother. "None of us did. You better come in."

"Thank you, madam. Dripping might pose a problem."

"It's only water," said my mother.

"Thank you, madam."

Together we all moved back, and the guy stood in our front hall, and dripping was a problem.

"So you're here to tell us about my husband's father?" said my mother. "You could have just written."

"Your father-in-law's passing is only part of my message, madam. I am to inform you as well that Mr. Seymour Jones has left a most generous endowment to support my continuing service to his family."

"I don't understand," said my mother.

"It seems reasonable to consider that a family with four young children and a father currently deployed in Germany might well stand in need of some aid suited to my occupation."

"You're here to help out?"

The guy gave another little bow. Really.

"While Jack's deployed?"

He nodded.

"Jack," she said. "Jack sent you."

"In a manner of speaking," said the guy.

My mother dropped That Look. She smiled. She started to bite her lip like she does when she's about to . . . Never mind.

"I can assure you, madam, my service in this capacity is exemplary, and I would gladly furnish names and addresses for reference, should you desire them."

"Wait," I said. "You mean my grandfather, like, left you to us in his will?"

"Crudely articulated, but true in the most generous sense."

"Like, we own you?"

The guy carefully tied shut the folds of his umbrella. "Young Master Jones, indentured servanthood having been abolished even in your country, no. You do not, like, own me."

"So," said Charlie, "you're a nanny?"

The guy's eyes opened wide.

"No, moron. He's not a nanny," I said.

"Jack sent a butler," my mother said, mostly to herself.

The guy cleared his throat. "I am most conservative about

such matters," he said. "I would very much prefer to be known as a gentleman's gentleman."

My mother shook her head.

"A gentleman's gentleman," she said. "Jack sent a gentleman's gentleman."

The guy bowed his little bow again.

"There's just one problem," she said. "There's no gentleman here."

Then the guy looked straight at me. Really. Straight at me. "Perhaps not yet," he said, and he handed me the satellite-disk umbrella.

That was how the Butler came into our house.

Can I just say, I wasn't so sure about this. I mean, he *said* he was a gentleman's gentleman—which, obviously, is a dumb way to say "butler"—but he could have been some kind of missionary in disguise. Or someone selling satellite-disk umbrellas. Or someone casing out our place for a burglary. Or a serial killer. Anything.

I could tell my mother wasn't so sure about him either.

That's why she thought for a long time when the Butler offered to drive us to school. When he asked, I whispered "Serial killer" to my mother, and she whispered "The fuel pump in the Jeep," and I whispered "Probably no ID," and she whispered "Raining hard"—and it was still raining like an Australian tropical thunderstorm—but I shrugged and whispered, "Does it matter to you if you never see us alive again?"

and that was really stupid because now she bit her lip hard and it was so really stupid because it was like I had forgotten that funeral.

So really stupid.

She closed her eyes for, like, a minute and then she opened them again and said she'd decided to go along with us to school, and the Butler nodded. My mother gave me a look—not That Look, but a look that said, "Don't let this guy out of your sight because maybe you're right and he really could be a serial killer," and then she went upstairs to get dressed.

So I was all over him when he opened up the four lunch bags and folded napkins into them—just to be sure he was putting in only napkins and not tracts or poison powder or anything like that. And I was still all over him when he finished Annie's hair and got the staples out of Charlie's new socks and pinned back Emily's bangs again because they had already come out.

You never know what a serial killer might do to throw you off-guard.

Ned would have been all over him too, but he was pretty excited, and like I told you, dachshunds throw up a lot—which he did again underneath the kitchen table after he sniffed the Butler's wet cuffs. The Butler started to wipe it up —I didn't need to be all over him while he was doing that—and when my mother came down and saw him under the kitchen table, she said he didn't come across the Atlantic to clean up after a dog, and he said, "Madam, the parameters of my duties are wide-ranging"—so my mother let him take care of Ned's throw-up and then we all went outside, sort of crowded together under the satellite-disk umbrella, which I was still holding.

My mother got in front and the four of us squeezed in the back, and we drove to school in the Butler's car, which was big and long and purple—like an eggplant. It had white-rimmed tires. It had running boards. On the front it had a chrome statue of someone who looked like she would be pretty cold in a stiff wind. It had pale yellow seats made of soft leather. And it also had, according to the Butler, "a properly placed steering mechanism"—even though it sure looked wrong to me.

So that's what we drove in to school instead of the Jeep.

When we dropped Annie off at the fifth-grade door, the Butler got out of the car, came around in the Australian tropical thunderstorm with his satellite-disk umbrella, opened the passenger door, and said, "Miss Anne, make good decisions and remember who you are."

"I will," she said.

My mother watched her run into the building. "I could have sworn I put her hair in two braids," she said.

"She preferred the one," said the Butler.

When we dropped Charlie off, the Butler opened the door and said, "Miss Charlotte, make good decisions and remember who you are," and Charlie held up her foot to show the Butler she was wearing her new bright yellow socks.

13

My mother told her to cut it out and get inside before she got soaked.

When we dropped Emily off, the Butler opened the door and said, "Miss Emily, make good decisions and remember who you are," and Emily asked if the Butler was going to pick us up in his purple car after school.

"No," I said.

My mother said, "Watch for the Jeep."

Then we drove to the middle school building, and while the Butler got out of the car, I got out too—before he could open my door. But he stood at the curb with his satellite-disk umbrella in the Australian tropical thunderstorm—the rain was splashing off the running boards—and he took off his bowler and said, "Make good decisions and remember who you are, young Master Jones." He put his bowler back on.

"You think I'm going to forget who I am?" I said.

"You are entering middle school now," he said. "I think it quite likely." Then he opened his door, folded his umbrella, and got inside again.

He drove off with my mother in the seat beside him. For a moment, I wondered if I would ever see her again.

I checked my front pocket for the green marble.

Then Billy Colt came up behind me, and he said, "Who was that?"

"Our butler," I said.

"You have a butler?"

The marble was there. "So?" I said.

We watched the purple car pull in front of a bus and drive away in the rain.

"His car looks like an eggplant," said Billy Colt.

"Yup."

"And he looks like a missionary."

"Yup," I said.

"Or a serial killer."

"That too."

Then we went inside to start our first day of sixth grade.

• 3 •

THE BOUNDARY

The perimeter of the field is generally lined in white chalk, setting the limits of play within this boundary.

OKAY, SO A LOT of the first day of sixth grade was pretty much what I expected. All the halls had new bulletin board displays that said WELCOME BACK, MINUTEMEN! and once we all got into our homerooms the loudspeaker came on and Vice Principal DelBanco welcomed everyone to school like it was the best thing in the whole world and wasn't everyone glad to be back at Longfellow Middle School and let's all give a big Longfellow Middle School welcome to all the new sixth graders because remember, seventh and eighth graders, you were once new sixth graders too! Then Principal Swieteck came on and she said she hoped we all would have a wonderful year and that she was eager to see all of us in our new classes—but she hoped she wouldn't see any of us in her office this year. (That was supposed to be a principal joke.)

Classes weren't as bad as I thought they were going to be. I got Mr. Barkus for Math Skills, and he showed us how he could memorize everyone's name, nickname, and street address after hearing them only once. I got Mrs. Harknet for homeroom, and she looked like she'd be okay—mostly because she had filled her classroom with more paperbacks than are in most libraries. The gym had that new gym smell and it was all ready for that first squeak across the glowing floor, even though Coach Krosoczka was patrolling the edges, making sure no sixth grader was stepping onto his floor wearing anything but sneakers. In the cafeteria, the lunch ladies had loaded strawberry milk into the coolers, which I'd never had before, but it seemed like a pretty good idea. In the science hall, Mrs. Wrubell had arranged glass beakers next to Bunsen burners so that her classroom looked like Frankenstein's lab and she told us we could try anything as long as we checked with her to make sure it wouldn't explode. Mr. Solaski told us we were now done with elementary school and he took education seriously and so should we—so he started right in teaching about the Boston Tea Party like he wasn't going to spend a minute not talking about American history. And I had Mrs. Harknet for Language Arts too, and she handed out textbooks that got printed, like, yesterday so the pages were still stuck together, but they looked all right even though they had poetry between the good parts.

So, pretty much what I expected—like shedding summer all day.

But there was one thing I hadn't expected.

Stupid Billy Colt told everyone about the Butler.

Everyone in the sixth grade.

All day long it was, "You have a butler? Really?"

And, "They still make butlers?"

And, "Is your butler going to carry your books to school?"

And, "Does your butler open your door for you and, like, bow all the time?"

And, "So does your butler tuck you in at night?"

That last one was from stupid Billy Colt, who almost got a face full of fist until I remembered who I was and made a good decision.

It helped that Vice Principal DelBanco was standing right there.

But when school was finally over and I was about to leave—and it was still raining an Australian tropical thunderstorm—I looked out the sixth-grade door and saw a whole crowd of sixth graders standing where the kids who get picked up stand, looking at something big and purple. Even kids who take the bus were standing there. So I walked over to the elementary building's fifth-grade door and I got Annie and we went around to the fourth-grade door and got Charlie and then we went to the second-grade door and found Emily and we stood there like giants around the second graders until the Butler came to pick us up.

My mother was in the front seat again.

We all squeezed in the back.

"How was your first day?" she said.

"I thought you were going to pick us up in the Jeep," I said.

"It's still in the shop," she said.

"I hope it won't be in the shop tomorrow."

"Young Master Jones . . ."

"Carter. My name is Carter. That's *Carter.*"

"So you did remember. Most gratifying. Young Master Jones, what you mean to say to your mother is 'And how was your day?'"

"What I mean to say is—"

"Because your mother has had a very long one, punctuated with unfortunate mechanical news of all stripes—if you'll pardon my interruption of your interruption."

"The Jeep?" I said.

"The Jeep is on its last legs," said my mother.

"Are you sure?"

The Butler looked over at me. "The mechanic's colloquial description of the situation was this: 'Lady, you can stick a fork in this one and call it done.'"

"So what are we going to do now?"

"Carter," my mother said, "let's just get home."

"Is the Jeep dead?" said Emily, in that voice that tells you she's about to cry.

"Don't be a baby," I said.

19

"I'm not a baby," she said.

"Carter," said my mother—with That Look.

So we drove home in the Eggplant, with the windshield wipers thumping back and forth, back and forth, back and forth—the only sound in the stupid purple car.

When we got back home, Ned was waiting for us—and he got pretty excited again and started bouncing around on his short legs and barking his high "Where have you been?" bark until he threw up. I figured this was a good time to take my backpack upstairs, but the Butler didn't think so.

"Young Master Jones," he said, and pointed.

"Aren't you supposed to do stuff like that?" I said.

"On the occasion of emergency. Had I been hired as your scullery maid—apparently with regularity. But I am not your scullery maid." He handed me a roll of paper towels and a plastic bag.

"Usually my mother—"

"Neither is your mother a scullery maid," said the Butler.

"So I am?"

"For such a time as this," said the Butler.

I took the roll of paper towels and the plastic bag.

I knelt down.

It was disgusting.

When I was finished, the Butler handed me Ned's leash.

"It's raining," I said.

The Butler went to the mudroom, brought back his satellite-disk umbrella, and handed it to me.

"I usually don't take Ned for walks right after school," I said. "I sort of like to crash."

"A habit confirmed by Ned's protruding belly. Isn't it fortunate that habits may be changed with discipline?"

"Mom," I said.

"Only around the block," she said.

"Around the block?" I said. "I'll be sopping wet when I get back."

Annie started to laugh.

"By which time Miss Anne will be well into her piano practice," said the Butler.

"I'm not taking piano lessons anymore," she said.

"A loss that you and I shall amend."

Annie no longer laughing.

"This isn't fair," I said.

"An irrelevancy," said the Butler.

"What does that mean?"

"It means that the claim of fairness is the consistent if unsympathetic whine of one who lives in a republic. A monarchist such as myself recognizes the virtue of simply getting to the thing that must be done. So, to it, young Master Jones."

I took Ned out.

The Australian tropical thunderstorm—which had thundered and stormed on and off all day—waited until we got out the door to start coming down sideways again. I didn't even try to use the satellite-disk umbrella. I figured that Ned would want to go back inside right away, so we'd only be out for like, a minute—but he didn't want to go back inside. He loved it. He ran through puddles up to his belly and let his ears blow straight behind him and kept his eyes mostly closed and his nose pointed up, and he watered the azaleas in front of the Ketchums' house and the rhododendrons in front of the Briggses' house and the holly hedge in front of the Rockcastles' house and the petunias in front of the Koertges' house, and then he pooped next to Billy Colt's driveway—which I figured stupid Billy Colt deserved for blabbing about the Butler—and then he went again in the day lilies on the other side of Billy Colt's driveway, and then we headed back since we were both starting to shiver and Ned couldn't have had anything left anyway after all he'd done.

And when we got home, the kitchen was warm as anything. There was a rag rug on the floor for Ned and a fluffy towel waiting for me and the Butler told me to go upstairs and put on dry clothes and then come right down. So I did, and when I came back into the kitchen there were hot chocolate chip cookies and a mug of something steaming.

"What's this?" I said.

"Tea with milk and sugar," said the Butler.

"I don't drink tea," I said.

"All civilized people drink tea, young Master Jones."

"Then I guess I'm not civilized."

"A claim you share with Vikings, Huns, assorted barbarian hordes, and marauders of all stripes. I have taken the liberty of adding more sugar than one might normally expect."

I sipped at it. I sipped again. It was pretty good.

"It stinks," I said.

The Butler sighed. "There is no need to announce repeatedly how very American you are."

"You know, I think I might know something about this, since I can remember who I am, but tell me if I'm wrong," I said. "We are in America, right? I mean, I'm supposed to be American, right?"

The Butler sighed again. "I think, young Master Jones, we will need to come to an understanding."

You bet, I thought.

⚬ 4 ⚬

TURN BLIND

When the batsmen ground their bats at the end of their run and change direction, the batsman facing the side of the field to which the ball has been struck must judge the likelihood of their making another successful run. When he turns in the opposite direction, or turns blind—a dangerous tendency—he cannot see the state of the play, and so takes the risk of being run out. To turn blind is a risky endeavor.

I DECIDED TO REVOLT. I mean, wiping up dog vomit, nearly drowning in an Australian tropical thunderstorm, drinking tea with milk and sugar—and it doesn't matter that I finished it, okay?—and I haven't even told you about the forty-five minutes of Mr. Barkus's word problems I had to do after Annie finished her stupid Chopin studies, forty-five minutes that were supposed to be thirty minutes but the Butler decided I needed to show my work on all the problems. And I'm not even going to talk about how he made me rewrite my one-paragraph description of "One Place I Went This Summer" for Mrs. Harknet four times—*four* times!—and how I had to check Emily's addition with her, even though no one ever checked my addition in second grade, and how I had to walk Ned around the block again before supper, and how I had to carry all my wet clothes to the washer and learn how to wash them myself, and how after all that I had to dry the dishes while the Butler scrubbed, and how before he left he made me promise to walk Ned one more time and put my clothes in the dryer and fold them. "Underwear as well, young Master Jones."

I mean, folding your stupid underwear?

How much can one person take?

So I decided to revolt.

But a revolt doesn't have to be obvious. I mean, it can start with a small thing. Something a British tyrant hardly even notices. But you open up a crack.

It's how we won the American Revolution, and remember: *that* all started with a little bit of tea.

So the next morning, when the Butler showed up on the stoop at 7:15, I opened the door, all smiles.

"Good morning," I said.

The Butler nodded. "Good morning, young Master Jones."

He stepped inside.

"My mom is upstairs with the girls," I said.

"Then I will see to lunches and to tea."

"Fine by me," I said. And when he was finished, there were four bags on the kitchen table, all neatly labeled: "Master Jones," "Miss Anne," "Miss Charlotte," "Miss Emily." And there were four mugs of tea with milk and sugar—which

Annie and Charlie and Emily chugged when they came downstairs.

"Do you want yours?" Emily said.

"No," I said.

"Can I have it?"

"No," I said.

"Can I give it to Ned?"

"Just leave it, Emily."

She stuck her tongue out.

I stuck my tongue out too.

My mother came down just before we had to leave. "Thank you so much."

"My pleasure, madam."

"You don't need to call me 'madam.'"

He looked at her.

"It's going to be 'madam,' isn't it?" she said.

"It is, madam."

"And what should *I* call *you*?" I said.

My mother and the Butler looked at me.

"Mr. Bowles-Fitzpatrick," said my mother.

"Mr. Bowles-Fitzpatrick?" I said.

"Yes, young Master Jones. Mr. Bowles-Fitzpatrick. And now, if the ladies would come along . . ."

"Bowles-Fitzpatrick?"

The Butler stopped and gave a long sigh. "You are such a very young nation, aren't you? And with so little sense of the persistence of history."

26

"Bowles-Fitzpatrick?" I said again.

Another sigh. "Bowles-Fitzpatricks fell in the Wars of the Roses long before you were a nation, and at least one fought with Nelson at the Battle of the Nile. Their latest martyrs include one who died in the trenches of Flanders during the First World War and one who died in a destroyer, accompanying the American merchant fleet during the Second. We are, as you might perceive, an aggressive lot, accustomed to battle. Be wary, young Master Jones. Now, ladies . . ."

We all bundled out to the Eggplant with umbrellas over us—the Butler had bought four new ones, all black—carrying our backpacks and our lunches.

And okay, maybe he was accustomed to battle and stuff. But I could be too. My father is a captain in the United States Army, after all.

So I left my lunch behind on the kitchen table. And the tea with milk and sugar too.

A revolt starts with a small thing.

The Butler—Mr. Bowles-Fitzpatrick—never noticed my lunch was missing the whole time we were driving to school. He didn't notice it was missing when I got out of the car— "Make good decisions and remember who you are." He didn't even notice when I waved and headed inside.

Later, when Mrs. Harknet asked where my lunch was, I told her I'd forgotten it but Billy Colt would split with me since he owed me for yesterday.

"I don't owe you for yesterday," said Billy Colt.

"You owe me for yesterday," I said.

"Is this about your butler?" he said.

"Do you want me to tell him you said he was a serial killer?"

"I didn't say he was a serial killer. I said he looked like a serial killer."

"You think serial killers care a whole lot about word choice?" I said.

So Billy Colt said he'd split with me. Then we turned in our one-paragraph descriptions, and Mrs. Harknet read through them with her laser teacher eyes and picked out three to read aloud to the whole class. As soon as she said she was going to do that, I knew she was going to read mine because the Butler made me write the thing over four times, you might remember, and who else in the whole sixth grade would have done that? So she read Patty Trowbridge's paragraph about an Amish farm in Pennsylvania, and Jennifer Washburn's paragraph about the aquarium in Chicago, and then she read about my visit to Liberty Park in New York City and how it was foggy and clammy and cold and we could hardly see anything until a wind came up off the river and suddenly it was clear and you could see the World Trade Center site and it was *solemn* (that word was the Butler's suggestion).

I guess you can tell the Butler wasn't a serial killer, since *he* cared about word choice.

"What wonderfully evocative connotations," said Mrs. Harknet.

28

"What wonderfully evocative connotations," whispered Billy Colt—who was probably mad about having to share his lunch.

"Shut up," I said.

And then Mrs. Harknet said for tonight we all had to write another one-paragraph description, this time about our room. "The paragraph should show something of yourself," said Mrs. Harknet. "You should do this not by direct statement, but by connotation."

"Your connotations are wonderfully evocative," whispered Billy Colt.

"Shut up," I said. "I mean it."

Mrs. Harknet told us to get started on our homework.

After that, science with Mrs. Wrubell, where we began our study of electrical ions—which doesn't sound all that exciting because it isn't all that exciting—and then PE, where Coach Krosoczka made us haul all the gray mats out of storage and into the yard to air them. "Cheap labor, boys," he said. "Cheap labor." The only thing that saved us from complaining was knowing that whoever was in seventh-period PE would have to haul them back inside.

But hauling mats is hungry work, so by the time we were going to eat, I was really hoping Billy Colt had a good-size lunch.

As it turned out, it didn't matter.

When we got to the cafeteria, kids were crowded around one of the tables, and when they saw us, someone hollered,

"There he is," and they all turned to look at me. You can imagine how weird that was. But then they parted, and I could see what they were gathered around.

A white linen tablecloth was draped over an end of one of the long cafeteria tables. On the white linen tablecloth was a white china plate with a thin gold band. On the right side of the plate was a knife and a spoon on top of a white linen napkin. On the left side were two forks. There was assorted citrus fruit in a small glass bowl above the plate, a salad in another glass bowl beside it, and little cruets of oil and vinegar. On the plate was a chicken breast with baby carrots and mushrooms. Parsley, too. Garlic bread steamed on another white china plate. A bottle of sparkling water was ready to pour into a glass over ice chips. Beside that, a china cup of hot tea with milk and sugar. And in front of it all was a white nameplate with "Master Carter Jones" in dark calligraphy.

"Dang," said Billy Colt. "So tomorrow, can I split with you?"

The Butler was really getting to be a pain in the glutes.

I decided I might have to be wary after all.

Whatever that meant.

• 5 •

THE PITCH

The pitch is the twenty-two-yard playing field between the wickets, on which all the action between the bowler and the batsmen must take place.

THAT NIGHT, my mother went to bed right after supper, and I worked on a one-paragraph description about my room that would show Mrs. Harknet something about myself not by direct statement but by connotation.

By the time the Butler had helped Emily read a story about a bunny looking for a home, and another story about a bunny with golden shoes, and two chapters of another story about a bunny named Edward—you get the theme here, right?—my floor was covered with balled-up pieces of paper, which the Butler saw when Charlie dragged him by my door on the way to showing him her books. I could hear them in her room, him saying, "Are you fond of E. Nesbit?" and Charlie saying, "Who?" and the Butler saying, "We shall stop by the library. Now, about your eleven and twelve times tables . . ." And when the eleven and twelve times tables were finished, Annie dragged the Butler by my door on their way to practicing Annie's spelling list of words that started with *pr,* and the Butler looked in at the mounds of balled-up pieces of paper and shook his head.

I could hear them practicing, and after Annie's progress providing and pronouncing practically every *pr* word in the language, the Butler proposed she prosper her study through prompt and profuse private attention to the list, and then he came to my room, where there was a whole landscape of balled-up pieces of paper.

"Progress seems preempted," he said.

"Stop that," I said.

"Apologies." He chose one of the balled-up pieces of paper and spread it out.

"I'm not very good at this," I said.

The Butler nodded.

"I mean, who gives stupid homework in the first stupid week of stupid school?"

The Butler balled up the piece of paper again. He picked up another, and he read it, and he balled it up again.

"A teacher whose primary aim is instruction," he said. "Are you meant to write about the antics of absurdly powerful characters in strangely colorful costumes?"

"I'm meant to write about my room. I'm describing those posters." I pointed.

The Butler nodded again. "Much more suitable to discuss than the unlaundered debris—which you will later attend to. But your sentences prattle on. Practicing economy, and preceding your verbs with some semblance of a proper subject, would—"

"You're doing it again."

"Apologies. I wonder if your teacher would be more interested in the details that say something about you, young Master Jones."

"Exactly. I'm supposed to write about how my room says something about me."

"So you are writing about superheroes."

"Yup."

"Then perhaps," said the Butler, "you might begin here." And he pointed at the photograph of my father, Captain Jackson Jonathan Jones, standing in front of an American flag.

"Or here." And he pointed at my father's beret from his first deployment in Iraq.

"Or here." And he pointed at the goggles that still had sand in them from Afghanistan.

And *stupid stupid stupid* I felt everything in me start to *stupid stupid stupid* go stupid watery.

"Write your first sentence," said the Butler.

I did.

"Please," he said, and he held out his hand. He took the paper and read it.

Then he read it out loud.

He read it out loud slowly: "My father is on the other side of the world, but he fills my room."

The Butler put the piece of paper back on my desk.

"I predict this beginning will not suffer the fate of its predecessors," he said.

He left.

It didn't.

Okay, so the next day, I remembered my lunch.

I was just being wary.

But Billy Colt was disappointed.

"So, the Butler isn't going to make . . ."

"No," I said.

"And there won't be any . . ."

"No," I said.

"You jerk," he said.

But at lunch, there was enough to share with Billy Colt anyway. It was almost like the Butler had planned for him, since there were two chive cream cheese sandwiches, two hard-boiled eggs, eight carrot sticks, and four small raisin scones.

"Tell your butler thanks," said Billy Colt. I think that's what he said. It's hard to speak with a whole hard-boiled egg in your mouth.

And Mrs. Harknet? She said my paragraph had plenty of wonderfully evocative connotations.

Plenty.

She told me I should email it to my father.

I decided I would.

On Friday, the Butler picked us all up in the Eggplant after school, and for the first time, my mother wasn't with him.

"Your mother," said the Butler, "is performing last rites for the Jeep."

"What does that mean?" said Emily.

"It means the Jeep's dead," said Annie.

"Jeeps don't die," said Emily.

"Indeed, they do not," said the Butler. "But they do finish their usefulness. Now, as it is Friday and gone three o'clock, I wonder if we might stop for a treat."

"A treat?" said Emily.

"Yes," said the Butler. "First, for Miss Emily and Miss Charlotte."

Emily and Charlie smiled the smiles they smile when they want to be pains in the glutes. But they were a little disappointed when the treat turned out to be a stop at the library to check out books by E. Nesbit for both of them.

"What does the *E* stand for?" said Charlie.

"'Excellent,'" said the Butler. "Miss Anne next."

Annie did not smile her pain-in-the-glutes smile, but she was a little disappointed too when the next stop was Madeleine's House of Music, where the Butler bought her a metronome.

"Is this really a treat?" she said.

"For all of us," said the Butler. "And it is worth noting that rhythm properly practiced"—he looked back at me, and I shook my head—"is important in all parts of life, but never more so than in music."

"Thanks," Annie said, not exactly like she was overwhelmed with happiness.

"Young Master Jones next," said the Butler.

And I have to say, when we stopped at Marysville Sports Shoppe, the possibilities for me looked a whole lot better than an E. Nesbit book and a metronome.

I mean, the words "Sports Shoppe" have lots of wonderfully evocative connotations.

The Butler told us to wait in the car and he would inquire about the special order he had made. So we waited, and I said to Annie, "Special order"—those words have lots of wonderfully evocative connotations too.

I think Annie tried a little bit not to hate me.

But when the Butler came back, he was carrying something long, and flat, and knobby at one end, and none of us could figure out what it was.

"It is," said the Butler, "what most everyone in the world, with the lamentable exception of the citizens of certain less civilized countries, would immediately recognize as a bat."

"That's not a bat," I said.

"You see my point. Young Master Jones, it *is* a bat in every part of the world where elegance is cherished, where communal memory is honored, where mannered people reign."

"We're mannered people," I said.

"Young Master Jones, last night you immersed your chocolate-glazed chocolate doughnut in your Coca-Cola."

"That's how you eat a chocolate-glazed chocolate doughnut," I said. "Obviously."

"And had I not intervened, you would have inserted the straw in your chocolate-flavored Coca-Cola into your left nostril."

Okay, that was true.

He handed me the bat.

"You are holding the wrong end, young Master Jones."

I turned it around. "Do I take the rope off?"

"Twine, and no."

I looked at the bat. "Can you play baseball with this?"

"Only if you were a savage."

"So what game can you play with it?"

The Butler's eyes almost closed. He began to smile. And he said, as if in a kind of trance, "The most lovely and sportsmanly game that mankind has yet conceived—or ever will conceive."

I looked at the bat again.

"Sure," I said.

"As you will remember, young Master Jones, mockery is the lowest form of discourse. Mockery of cricket, however, is akin to blasphemy, and will not be spoken in my presence."

The way he said it, I knew he wasn't kidding.

"So, what kind of wood is this?" I said, like I cared.

"Willow," said the Butler. "And tonight, you shall knock it in."

And if you don't know what "knock it in" means, you've obviously never held a new cricket bat and had a butler give you a small bottle of linseed oil and a clean rag, and then rubbed the oil into the wood, and rubbed it in, and rubbed it in, and rubbed it in while he watched, his hands moving to show you how to do it, like he probably did it when he was a kid, like he was probably wanting to do it himself now. And then you bang a cricket ball all over the bat so the wood gets roughed up. The Butler thought it was some big rite or something that I should go through.

But you know what? I wasn't thinking of it being a rite.

I was thinking how much my brother Currier would have loved this.

He would have spilled linseed oil everywhere, but dang, he would have loved it.

By the way, after I finished lunch that day, I went to the school library and emailed my paragraph with wonderfully evocative connotations to my father. Then I checked my email on one of the library computers just before we left school.

But that's how it is when you're deployed, right? I mean, maybe he didn't get the email. Or maybe he was out on a mission. Or maybe it was really late at night there. Or maybe they were on lockdown or something and the base had gone dark because of an imminent threat.

There's a ton of reasons why he might not be able to write back.

A ton.

∘ 6 ∘

THE UMPIRE

The umpire is the ultimate arbiter of fair play, from the moment when the coin is tossed to begin the game through the final counting of the runs. An expert on the rules of cricket, the umpire brings to the contest fairness, close observation, and a sense of the game's tradition.

MY MOTHER WAS standing outside the open garage when we got home. The empty open garage.

"Is the Jeep really dead?" said Emily.

"I'm afraid so," said my mother.

"So are we going to get another one?"

My mother closed the garage door, and suddenly I got it.

There wasn't going to be another Jeep.

For the same reason we'd never gotten another micro-wave when the glass in the old one blew out.

For the same reason I gave my bike to Annie and never got another one.

For the same reason we had a computer so old it couldn't play games—which we didn't have anyway so it didn't matter.

For the same reason Annie and Emily and Charlie got new sneakers for school but I didn't.

"Miss Emily," said the Butler, "I will be your transportation for the present."

"You're going to drive us in the Eggplant every day?"

"I will drive you in the Bentley every day, Miss Emily— until such time as young Master Jones has his own license."

You know how much it stinks to begin the first week of sixth grade with sneakers from the middle of fifth grade? You know how much tread they have left?

"Carter can't drive," said Emily.

The Butler raised one eyebrow.

It really stinks.

"Young Master Jones," the Butler said, and he pointed to the Eggplant.

"What?" I said.

He walked to the door and opened it. The door on the driver's side.

"What?" I said again.

"If you will get in, we will adjust the seat."

I looked at my mother. She shrugged, gathered the girls, and moved back toward the house.

I got in. The Butler went around and got in the other side.

"I'm twelve years old," I said.

"Then there's no time to lose. Do you know which is the accelerator and which the brake?"

I nodded.

"The clutch?"

I looked around by my feet, and nodded.

"And the gearstick?"

Nodded again.

He handed me the keys. "You begin by engaging the ignition." He pointed. "That key, inserted there." I inserted it. "Now turn and release as soon as the ignition has caught." I did, and the Eggplant thrummed beneath me.

Okay, so this didn't stink. This was pretty cool.

Emily, Charlie, and Annie had reached the front stoop. My mother had her arms around them. You know how in *Ace Robotroid and the Robotroid Rangers* some characters look at Ace Robotroid with their mouths opened up wide as caverns because of how amazing he is?

That's what Emily and Charlie were doing. Annie, not so much.

"I don't really know how to do this," I said.

"You are getting ready to put the Bentley into R for . . ."

"'Reverse,'" I said.

"Excellent. Put your left hand on the gearstick."

I did. The Butler put his hand over mine.

"Press down on the clutch."

I pressed down.

"And now put the gearstick into reverse."

I did.

"And using your right foot, gently press down on the

accelerator and gently lift your foot off the clutch until you feel the engine bite."

I pressed down on the accelerator and lifted my foot off and felt the engine bite.

"We shall discuss the meaning of the word 'gently' another time. Now, release the handbrake."

I did, and I felt the Eggplant purr in readiness.

It was so cool.

"Look back over your left shoulder. Good. Now lift up slightly on the clutch again, press down slightly on the accelerator, hold the wheel quite straight . . ."

I did—and the Eggplant rolled back along the driveway with the smooth power of a planet in its orbit.

"If you continue turning in that direction, young Master Jones, you will reposition the row of hostas. Thank you. Exactly right. That should relieve your mother's mind considerably."

We passed the row of hostas.

"And you will be mindful of the black walnut tree at the end of the drive?"

I was mindful of the black walnut tree at the end of the drive.

"Engage the brake, please," said the Butler.

I did.

"Well done. Shall we do it properly and take the Bentley once round the block?" he said.

I nodded.

"Back out into the road, please. Wait to turn. Wait. Wait. Now, young Master Jones. Nicely done. Straighten the wheel. And there you have it. Prepare to change gear, and then press down lightly upon the accelerator."

And I did have it. And I did prepare to change gear. And I did change. And okay, so the Eggplant stalled. But I started it again, and I pressed down lightly on the accelerator, and the Eggplant rolled forward. And I turned the corner and we drove past the Ketchums' azaleas and the Briggses' rhododendrons and the Rockcastles' holly hedge and the Koertges' petunias and Billy Colt's house—you can't believe how much I wanted Billy Colt to be outside to see me, but he wasn't— and around the next corner, the Eggplant thrumming and purring beneath me and sometimes the Butler's hand on mine to help with the steering but mostly not.

And when we got home, the girls and my mother were all standing on the front stoop with Ned, still watching like in *Ace Robotroid and the Robotroid Rangers*—even Ned.

We stopped in the driveway since my mother had closed the garage door. I put the Eggplant into neutral. I turned off the ignition. I took out the keys and handed them to the Butler. We got out. Emily and Charlie and even Annie clapped. My mother smiled this weird smile, like I had just grown up or something. Talk about rites! Even Ned was pretty excited—and you already know what happens when Ned gets excited.

"Well done, young Master Carter. Very well done, indeed."

"It is such a cool car."

"Your grandfather would have agreed, though his diction might have differed. When it was clear he would no longer have need of it, he himself arranged to have it shipped across the ocean for you—one of the last tasks he was able to complete."

"Wait—for me?"

"The Bentley is yours, young Master Carter. I have its use only until you come of age."

"When's that?"

"On the day you celebrate your eighteenth birthday."

"That's like a million years from now."

"Actually, it is nothing like a million years from now. It is a short six years from now. And in the meantime, there is enough to occupy you that hardly requires a Bentley— as, for example, Ned's deposit—or, even more pressing, the elimination of the use of *like* as an adverb from your vocabulary."

I took care of Ned's deposit, and after that, I took Ned for a walk around the block, and he calmed down after he pooped by Billy Colt's driveway.

But I didn't calm down. Not for a whole long while.

I drove the Eggplant!

I drove the Eggplant!

I really, like, drove the Eggplant!

I mean, I really drove the Eggplant!

Which I would own once I came of age.

And when I got back to the house, I said to the Butler, "Thanks, Mr. Bowles-Fitzpatrick. Are you sure it isn't sixteen?"

The Butler smiled a little and said, "Quite sure, young Master Carter. Now, as you are here, Miss Anne is struggling with setting the timing on her metronome. Perhaps some brotherly assistance would be apt."

So I gave her some brotherly assistance. Just this once.

That night, after hamburgers and french fries—and I ate my french fries with a fork just to show how mannered I was, and I didn't even say anything about how Mr. Bowles-Fitzpatrick ate his french fries with vinegar instead of ketchup like any civilized person is supposed to do—my mother asked the Butler where he was staying.

"Thank you, madam," he said. "I have taken rooms let by Mr. Krebs, just a few blocks from—"

"Carson Krebs's father?" I said.

"I believe so, yes. Perhaps you know the boy?"

"Not really."

"A young lad who has had to grow up rather quickly," said the Butler.

My mother nodded. "Are the rooms . . ." My mother hesitated, and I know what she wanted to ask. My father had a study downstairs, with a pullout couch and a bathroom down the hall. She looked like she was wondering what I was wondering: Wouldn't it be easier if Mr. Bowles-Fitzpatrick just moved in?

"The arrangement suits everyone well," the Butler said.

And the moment passed. I have to say, it sort of surprised me that I suddenly felt disappointed.

But you know what moment didn't pass?

You know what moment I couldn't stop thinking about?

I drove the Eggplant!

I drove the Eggplant!

I really, like, drove the Eggplant!

A TRUE WICKET

A true wicket is a flat pitch where the cricket ball bounces in a very predictable way — the opposite of a sticky wicket.

AFTER HE LEFT that night, we wondered if the Butler would come on Saturday too — even though, my mother said, he must want some time off. But on Saturday morning, when I got up for *Ace Robotroid and the Robotroid Rangers,* the Butler was already in the kitchen, humming.

"Let me guess," I said. "Beethoven."

"Elgar," said the Butler. "Beethoven is too German for mornings."

I went to the pantry to get breakfast.

I looked through all the boxes of cereal.

No Ace Robotroid Sugar Stars.

I looked again.

No Ace Robotroid Sugar Stars.

How can you watch *Ace Robotroid and the Robotroid Rangers* with no Ace Robotroid Sugar Stars?

I pulled out most of the cereal on the cereal shelf to make sure—even the cereal that is so healthy that no one ever eats it.

No Ace Robotroid Sugar Stars.

"They're not there," called the Butler. I went back into the kitchen, where he was dicing onions and red peppers.

"What aren't there?"

"Uncivilized Sugar Stars."

"Just because they don't have Ace Robotroid Sugar Stars in Buckingham Palace doesn't mean they're uncivilized," I said.

"Yes, it does," said the Butler, and he scraped the onions and red peppers into a bowl of whisked eggs.

Okay, this was really getting to be a pain in the glutes.

Driving the Eggplant was great. But that didn't make up for the Ace Robotroid Sugar Stars. I mean, Ace Robotroid Sugar Stars didn't seem like a whole lot to ask for after a week of sixth grade.

Probably the Butler hadn't even tried Ace Robotroid Sugar Stars.

Probably he'd never even heard of Ace Robotroid Sugar Stars before.

"So what am I supposed to eat for breakfast?"

"A tray is poised for your arrival in the dining room," he said.

I went into the dining room. A glass of orange juice. An egg sitting in a little cup with a little knitted cap on—to keep it warm, I guess. Two pieces of toast standing in a rack. A dollop of orange marmalade—I hate orange marmalade—in a white bowl. Salt and pepper shakers. A quartered pear. And a cup of tea with milk and sugar, the saucer on top to keep it warm too.

"This is going to be hard to eat in front of *Ace Robotroid and the Robotroid Rangers*," I called into the kitchen.

"Imagine the relief you must feel, knowing you need not eat your breakfast in front of *Ace Robotroid and the Robotroid Rangers*, but may eat it in the dining room, like a—"

"I know, I know: like a civilized person."

"Indeed."

This was really, really getting to be a pain in the glutes.

I sat down in the dining room. No one else was up yet, but I sat down in the dining room. By myself. In the dining room. Where we never eat. The dining room.

You know how weird it is to sit in a dining room when you're the only one there?

I took the knitted cap off the egg.

"How am I supposed to eat this egg?" I hollered.

"One places the knife against the shell, parallel with the lip of the cup. Apply pressure gradually and the shell will open up. Then—"

"Got it," I said.

I placed the knife against the shell, parallel with the lip of the cup. I applied pressure gradually.

The shell did not open up.

I applied more pressure gradually.

The shell did not open up.

More pressure gradually.

And more.

Not gradually.

Until the knife ripped through the stupid egg and the top half slopped over the white bowl of orange marmalade and plopped onto the floor.

I am not making this up.

Onto the floor.

Fortunately, Ned was by the table to lap up the egg.

"All perfectly well in there, young Master Carter?"

"Perfectly," I said.

I ate the bottom half of the egg and tried not to mind the pieces of eggshell. I ate the toast without the marmalade. I drank the tea, which had plenty of milk and sugar in it. When I was done, I picked up the eggshells Ned had left on the floor and scratched behind his ears to thank him for taking care of the plopped egg.

Then he threw up.

"You'll need to take Ned for his walk soon," the Butler called.

"So would it have killed you to wait?" I said—but just to Ned.

‿ ‿ ‿

I took Ned for his walk anyway. The second time around the block, Billy Colt was waiting for us. He pointed at Ned.

"Does he always poop next to my driveway?"

"Always," I said. "I trained him to do it."

"Don't you have a butler to do this?"

"Do what?"

"Pick it up or something?"

"Only on the occasion of an emergency—and this isn't."

"Maybe not to you," he said.

"Exactly," I said.

Billy Colt tilted his head. "Is he throwing up, too?"

"Did you see the Butler's car drive by yesterday?"

"No."

"You sure? Like, around four o'clock?"

"No. How come?"

"No reason," I said—and I was sort of surprised at how disappointed I was.

Not as much as I was about not getting an email back, though.

8

A RABBIT

A rabbit is a batsman who may be new to the game — or simply not very skilled — and so seems to be fearful as he faces the bowler.

BY THE TIME I got back home, the kitchen was smelling of apples, and my mother and Emily and Charlie and Annie were standing around the kitchen table eating little apple tarts for breakfast, and then Billy Colt and I were eating little apple tarts too — I'd told him he could come home to eat breakfast with us if I didn't have to pick up the you-know-what. We were all drinking big glasses of milk — "Is this one percent?" said Billy Colt. "Certainly not," Emily said — and when we were all done and we'd gathered up the dishes, the Butler said, "Right. Give me a moment and we'll be off."

Billy Colt looked at me. "Off where?"

I shrugged.

The Butler tossed me the Eggplant's keys and said,

"Would you mind warming up the Bentley, young Master Carter?"

Billy Colt looked at me again.

"Sure," I said.

"And young Master William, if you would be so good as to carry in the long case and the rather cumbersome bag you'll find on the back seat, I'd be so grateful."

We went out to the Eggplant and I started her thrumming, then went back inside. Billy brought in the case and the rather cumbersome bag and said, "You ever drive it?" and I said, "All the time," and he said, "Where?" and I said, "Around," and he said he wished he had a butler too, and then the Butler came out of the bathroom.

He wasn't in his suit anymore.

He was all in white: white shoes, white long pants, white collared shirt, white sweater over the white collared shirt, a white hat. He took the rather cumbersome bag from Billy Colt, opened it, and took out two huge marshmallowy pads.

Billy and I stared at the pads, sort of stunned.

"Young Master Carter," he said, "if you own a white collared shirt, this would be a good time to put it on."

I went upstairs. I did have a white collared shirt, you know, because that's what you wear to funerals. And I'd been to one, like I said.

"And if you would fetch your bat," the Butler called after me.

When I came back downstairs, the Butler and Billy were

outside. The Butler had put down the marshmallowy pads and he was rummaging around in the long case. He pulled out two white sweaters and two white hats.

"We will have to make do with these, though they may be a bit on the large side. Don them, please."

What could we do? We donned them, and by the time we were finished putting on white sweaters and white hats, Annie and Charlie and Emily—who were on the stoop—had almost collapsed, giggling.

"You should wear those all the time," said Charlie.

"Shut up," I said.

The sweaters were a little too long and the hats were too big, but maybe they were supposed to look like that. Anyway, the Butler didn't seem to notice.

"Mr. Bowles-Fitzpatrick, what are you supposed to be?" said Annie.

The Butler rummaged around in the long case again and took out two huge gloves—white, again—and he handed them to Billy. "Try these on," he said. Then he looked back at Annie. "Miss Anne, I am not *supposed* to be anything. I *am* a cricketer."

"A cricketer?"

"Of some skill."

Annie pointed to Billy Colt and me—Billy still trying to adjust the gloves that came halfway up to his elbows.

"And what are they supposed to be?"

The Butler pointed at Billy Colt. "To begin, the batsman."

55

He pointed to me. "The fielder." He pointed to himself. "The bowler."

I started to sweat, and not just because of the white sweater.

"If we're playing cricket, where are we supposed to go?" I said.

"Your school field seems the reasonable option," said the Butler.

I looked at the white sweater and the white hat Billy Colt was wearing. He looked at the white sweater and the white hat I was wearing. We looked at the marshmallowy pads. The gloves. The white hats again.

"No, we're not going to school," I said.

"Indeed we are," said the Butler.

"I have to go home for lunch now," said Billy Colt.

"Not at all," said the Butler, "though we will need to stop to inform your parents of your whereabouts."

"I'm going to be sick," said Billy Colt.

"You are not a dachshund," said the Butler. He picked up the long case and looked up at the sky. "After all, I think we shall walk. Young Master Carter, if you will turn off the car."

"We're not going to drive there?"

"It is a very short walk, and the day is lovely and warm."

I looked at the white sweater and the white hat Billy Colt was wearing. He looked at the white sweater and the white hat I was wearing. We looked at the marshmallowy pads. The gloves. The white hats again.

"Someone might see us," I said.

Billy Colt nodded.

"And if you were doing something shameful, you would be properly embarrassed. However, since cricket is a game internationally played and internationally broadcast—as opposed to the insular, provincial, and misnamed football games played in this country—you must feel you are embarking upon a great global tradition."

"Yup, that's exactly how I feel," I said.

"Excellent," said the Butler, "remembering that mockery is—"

"I know," I said.

"What does *provincial* mean?" said Billy.

"American," said the Butler. He started on ahead of us.

"Just hope there's no one at school," I whispered to Billy Colt.

But of course there was. You knew there would be.

9

THE CREASE

The crease is the playing area into which the batsman steps when he is about to protect his wicket.

I TOLD YOU I've been to Australia, right? And how it rained Australian tropical thunderstorms almost every day—which my father said wasn't all that unusual. The last time he'd been to Australia, he said, it had rained *every* day.

I went with my father the summer before fifth grade because we had some ancestors who were sent to the penal colonies in Australia in seventeen something something and my father wanted to track them down for the family's history. Plus we'd get to see places he'd seen just after college.

That's the reason he gave when he told me we were going.

I don't think that was the real reason.

I think the reason was that my mother told him he should spend some time with me because of how it was after my brother Currier . . . you know. I think she told him he had to do it and she didn't care if he had to call in some favors from the army. I think she told him that she didn't give a flying leap about duty and crap like that—his son needed him.

Our house has thin walls.

Anyway, I think that's the reason we went to Australia.

But it didn't matter why we went. I mean, Australia! I put the green marble in my pocket and we went to the airport in a taxi and we flew for a bazillion hours to Los Angeles and then another bazillion bazillion hours to Australia and in the middle of the night we watched movies I don't think my mom would have let me watch if she had been there.

We landed in Sydney and got in a car with the steering wheel on the wrong side like the Eggplant and drove out of the city on the wrong side of the road and came to the Blue Mountains, which didn't look blue at all. It was already tropical thunderstorming. But my father didn't care. He wanted to hike before we looked up ancestors, so we shouldered backpacks—his was a lot heavier than mine—and we climbed down to the valley floor. Small waterfalls all around us. Trees getting thicker and thicker. High rocks and long red layers of sandstone. The smell of wet earth and water and big leaves and damp moss and old bark and huge white flowers I'd never seen before.

A thousand feet down, we set off into the big trees, him humming Beethoven while we hiked—and he could do whole symphonies, even in the Australian tropical thunderstorm.

Where we walked, we left deep tracks that filled with rainwater. It was hot. Sounds of water falling onto rocks. The screeching of white birds that flocked high up in the tall trees and stared down at us. Every so often a hunting call from something big—like a dinosaur, maybe. Every so often something slithering in the low grass—probably snakes, my father said. Every so often something scrambling through the underbrush—probably little crocodiles, my father said.

They didn't sound little.

And then, in the late afternoon, the rain stopped and the sun sprang out from behind puff clouds and we came to a clearing that gave away the whole valley.

"Watch," said my father.

The sunlight belted the leaves of the eucalyptus trees and steam began to rise up, and up, and up, and no kidding, the air turned blue. Blue over the leaves, blue over the tallest trees, blue over the red rock formations, blue hovering everywhere, and then blue coming down onto us. I could almost hold my hand out and watch it turn blue.

Blue.

We saw it happen every afternoon, when the Australian tropical thunderstorm stopped and the sunlight hit the trees and their eucalyptus oils evaporated into the air and everything hovered blue.

We were down in the valley for five days. We never saw another person the whole time.

We were just there. My father and me. Just there. Just us.

We didn't even talk that much.

Hardly at all.

It was so quiet, I almost missed Annie and Charlie and Emily.

And I held the green marble tightly.

And now, walking with the Butler, in a white sweater and a white hat carrying marshmallowy pads and huge gloves and a bat that wasn't really a bat, it's where I kind of wished I still was.

We walked past the Ketchums—who were watering their azaleas and who looked up and stared at us—past the Briggses' rhododendrons, past the Rockcastles' holly hedge, past the Koertges' petunias—the Koertges stared at us out the window—and stopped by Billy Colt's house, where he tried to tell his mother he was feeling sick because he ate too many apple tarts but the Butler told Mrs. Colt we'd be learning to play cricket and she told Billy it was a wonderful opportunity and he looked like such a little gentleman in his white sweater and white hat, and we walked six more blocks to Longfellow Middle School.

"You look like such a little gentleman," I said.

"Shut up," Billy Colt said.

And I don't know where Billy Colt wished he was, but I could bet it wasn't on the Longfellow Middle School fields, where three pickup games were already going.

Three pickup games, on the three baseball diamonds that

butted up against the red oval of the track, where the eighth-grade varsity cross-country team was getting timed by Coach Krosoczka, who was hollering like he was not a very happy coach.

We crossed the track, hesitated, then followed the Butler onto the perfect green lawn of the Longfellow Middle School football field, home of the Longfellow Middle School Minutemen, a lawn cut and watered and fertilized and worshiped by a whole team of landscapers, a lawn watched over like it was holy ground by Vice Principal DelBanco—who was the football coach when he wasn't being the vice principal—a lawn upon which no sixth grader had ever stepped before.

I was sweating.

"This will do perfectly," said the Butler.

"Mr. Bowles-Fitzpatrick . . ."

"Keep up, young Master William."

Billy Colt was sweating too.

We followed the Butler to the center of the Longfellow Middle School football field. I turned around and looked at the baseball diamonds. One of the left fielders was looking our way.

The Butler took three long stakes out of his case—and a wooden hammer.

"Mr. Bowles-Fitzpatrick," I said, "you can't . . ."

The Butler pounded the first stake in.

"Mr. Bowles-Fitzpatrick, you really can't . . ."

He pounded in the second. Then the third. I turned around again. Most of the outfielders from all three diamonds were looking at us now.

"Mr. Bowles-Fitzpatrick," I said again.

He reached into the case, pulled some stuff out, put it back again, and finally held up two short pieces of wood. "These are called the bails," he said. "Repeat after me, please. 'The bails.'"

"'The bails,'" we said, sort of helplessly.

He laid them carefully across the tops of the stakes, and then, pointing at the stakes, the Butler said, "These are called the stumps. Please repeat."

"'The stumps.'"

"Young Master William, together the stumps and the bails are the wicket. You are standing in what is called the crease. A good cricketer stands in the crease to defend his wicket to the death. So, put on your pads—you'll have to lay the gloves aside for the moment—yes, that's right. Put on the pads—you'll need to help him, young Master Carter. And then"—rummaging about in the case again—"remove your hat and replace it with this." He handed Billy a black hat with something like a cage on the front.

Billy tried it on.

"No, that's not quite right. Let me help you."

I looked around again. Two of the pickup games had stopped to look at us.

"All right, then," said the Butler. "Young Master William,

you take the bat and hold it by the handle—both hands—yes. And now you'll stay here in the crease and young Master Carter and I will take a bit of a walk."

Billy Colt looked around behind him, then at all the outfielders from the three pickup games, then back at us. "You're not going to leave me here," he said.

"It is your wicket to defend to the death."

Billy did sort of look like death was on his mind.

"Now, young Master Carter, we walk twenty-two yards precisely. How nice that the yardage is so clearly marked."

"The reason the yardage is so clearly marked is that this is the football field and we're not supposed to be on it."

"Fifteen, sixteen, seventeen, eighteen, nineteen, twenty, twenty-one, twenty-two," the Butler counted. He laid the case down again and took out three more stumps and two bails. "Presumably your family pays its city taxes?" he said. He handed the bails to me and began to pound the first stump in. "Given such financial faithfulness, we might assume you may freely walk onto a publicly owned school field." He pounded in the second stump.

I turned around. All three games had stopped.

They were all looking at us.

Coach Krosoczka and the eighth-grade varsity cross-country team were looking at us too.

"I'm not sure everyone understands that," I said.

"Then perhaps," said the Butler, pounding in the third

stump, "a stronger emphasis on the study of civics and democracy is required at Longfellow Middle School."

Coach Krosoczka began walking toward us.

Coach Krosoczka did not look interested in a stronger emphasis on the study of civics and democracy.

Behind Coach Krosoczka came the entire eighth-grade varsity cross-country team. Twelve eighth graders.

They didn't look like they were interested in a stronger emphasis on the study of civics and democracy either.

I told you how in the Blue Mountains of Australia my father and I were surrounded by screeching birds and hunting dinosaurs and slithering snakes and scrambling crocodiles?

I think it might have been safer there than it was right now on the football field of Longfellow Middle School.

• 10 •

THE WICKETKEEPER

The wicketkeeper plays behind the batsman and wicket to catch the balls that the batsman misses. He stands closer to or farther from the wicket depending upon the speed of the bowler. He wears protective gloves—the only fielder to do so.

BILLY WAS STILL standing by the other wicket. I thought I heard him whimper from twenty-two yards away. The eighth-grade varsity cross-country team would reach him first.

"Place the bails on the stumps, please," said the Butler.

I did.

The Butler rummaged again in the case. He pulled out a red ball and tossed it lightly up and down in his hand. He looked at Billy.

"Now, young Master William, it is my role to bowl this ball, bouncing it once, so that it hits your wicket, knocking off the bails. It is your role to defend your wicket, batting the ball away so that it reaches into this area around the pitch. You will then run to the wicket behind me—no, young Master Carter, this one—to score one run. If you can make it back to where you started, you will score two runs. Had we another batsman working with you, he would start at the stumps behind me, and you would cross over and trade places with each run, together scoring runs until such time as young Master Carter—who will represent the entire fielding team—had retrieved the ball and brought it in. Do you understand?"

Billy Colt nodded, but I doubted he understood a single thing.

"Do you understand?" the Butler said to me.

I nodded too—but I really didn't understand a single thing.

The eighth-grade varsity cross-country team had grouped behind Billy Colt. They watched their coach walk the twenty-two yards toward us.

Now I was sure Billy was whimpering.

The Butler turned back to Billy. "Young Master William, your rather anxious expression suggests that there are some elements of the game that yet seem unclear."

Billy nodded again.

The Butler turned back to me. "Perhaps it would be best if you took the bat first, young Master Carter."

I looked at the Butler. I looked at the eighth-grade varsity cross-country team coach coming toward us. I looked at the eighth-grade varsity cross-country team gathered around Billy Colt at the wicket he was supposed to defend to the death.

"What?" I said.

"Inform young Master William that he will field at point."

"Okay," I said.

"And perhaps this scowling gentleman advancing with such purpose will be wicketkeeper."

The scowling gentleman advancing with such purpose did not look at all like he wanted to be wicketkeeper.

"Mr. Bowles-Fitzpatrick, I don't think so."

"Nonsense." The Butler steadied the bails on top of the stumps. "On a brisk morning such as this one, who could resist the opportunity to be wicketkeeper?"

"I can't imagine," I said.

"Hey, you!" said Coach Krosoczka. "What do you think you're doing?"

He really did not sound like he wanted to be wicketkeeper.

The Butler finished steadying the bails. He slowly lifted his hands from the wicket, then turned to the coach.

"At the moment," he said, "I am preparing to play one of the world's most elegant sports. Equally, I am hoping you might be wicketkeeper."

This stopped Coach Krosoczka.

"Excuse me?" he said.

"No excuse necessary. Young Master William has the gloves. Come with me and I will show you where to stand."

"Where to stand?"

We started walking back the twenty-two yards toward Billy Colt. Coach Krosoczka came with us.

"To the left and back from the wicket," said the Butler. "I'd suggest you stand only slightly back, as we will not be bowling with anything like speed today. I am sorry—perhaps you are already familiar with the game?"

Coach Krosoczka looked like he was not as sure of himself as he wanted to be. "What game is it?"

"Cricket," said the Butler, "and no matter. A sportsman such as yourself, it will come to you quickly. And you gentlemen"—he was calling to the eighth-grade varsity cross-country team now—"you gentlemen—young Master Krebs, good to see you—would you rotate once please?"

They looked at the Butler.

"Just once. Clockwise, if you please."

After a moment, they all rotated once. Clockwise.

"How convenient to have your names printed so prominently on your jerseys. Young Master Krebs—yes, it all comes back, doesn't it?—young Masters Krebs and Hopewell—a most forward-thinking name—you will be slips, and you will stand here and here around the pitch. No, young Master Hopewell, here. We need keen eyes and quick hands at gully—perhaps young Master Singh? Splendid. Young Master Chall, you look like sprinting may be in your blood. Shall we say that you will field at point with young Master William? Be ready, for the ball may come at you quickly—but it is also a lovely position from which to learn the game. Young Masters Jenkins and Briggs—not related to the Thornton-Briggs, are you? I suppose not—you will be covers and stand here and here. You, young Master Hettinga, are at midwicket—here. Young Master Bryan, at mid-off—here. And so you see, gentleman, we have fanned out in such a way as to cover the entire field and are now prepared to deal with any ball that comes off the bats of the opposing team. Now, young Masters Carter, de la Pena, Klatt, Barkus, and Yang—who together sound much like a firm of solicitors—you will represent that opposing team and prepare to bat. Young Masters Carter and Barkus, you are the first batsmen, I will bowl the overs, and Coach . . ."

"Krosoczka," said the cross-country coach.

"Coach Krosoczka will be wicketkeeper for both teams."

Coach Krosoczka was still sort of scowling, and he still did not seem like he wanted to be wicketkeeper for both teams, but he took up his position to the left and about four steps back from the wicket.

"Perhaps a little closer, Coach Krosoczka."

Coach Krosoczka came one step closer.

"Splendid all around. Now, young Master Carter, you will need those pads on your thighs. Young Master Krebs, if you would lend him assistance for a moment."

Carson Krebs, who is the captain of the eighth-grade varsity cross-country team, took the pads that Billy Colt handed him. Together, we strapped them on my legs.

"Do you know what you're doing?" he said.

Those, by the way, were probably the first words that

Carson Krebs, eighth grader, had ever spoken to a sixth grader at Longfellow Middle School.

"What?"

"Do you know what you're doing?"

"Nope," I said.

"This is cricket," he said.

"I know."

"Then you know you don't fool around with cricket, right?"

"Right."

"So pay attention," he said.

Everything in me suddenly froze. I thought I heard high screeches from far away.

"What?"

"Cricket is serious. Pay attention."

"And while they are negotiating the pads," said the Butler, "let me instruct you all in your duties." And he did. One by one. Gully and slips and covers and the midwicket and the point fielder and the mid-off and even the wicketkeeper.

I couldn't figure out why Carson Krebs wanted me to pay attention to whatever it was I was doing, which I wasn't sure about anyway, so how would I even know if I screwed up? And what did he care?

"We will practice our batting only at this point. Running between the wickets will come later—though young Master Barkus, to give us some sense of the lovely camaraderie necessitated by this game, perhaps you would take your place at the wicket behind me, imagining a run across the pitch if young Master Carter were to strike well."

"Okay," Barkus said—even though I don't think he knew what he was doing either.

The Butler walked toward the other wicket, then turned.

"Young Master Carter, are you ready?" he called.

"He's ready," said Carson Krebs.

No, I wasn't.

"How about if Barkus goes first?" I said.

"You've already got the pads on," said Krebs.

I turned back to the Butler. I held the bat up. I could still smell the linseed oil.

"All right, then," said the Butler. "Bat straight, young Master Carter. Straight, not bent, when you strike the ball. And head still, not bobbing about as if it were on a spring. Feet a little farther apart. Young Master Krebs, perhaps you will show him. Exactly right."

The Butler turned to the eighth-grade varsity cross-country team. "Remember, a keen eye. You are either catching the ball or racing to the boundary—which we will define as your sidelines for the sake of convenience—to retrieve the ball and throw it back to the bowler or wicketkeeper. Soft hands, all around. And as I run in to deliver the ball, you would all do well to take one or two steps toward the batsman. This is not meant to intimidate as much as it is meant to show your active awareness."

"You got all that?" hollered Coach Krosoczka.

The whole eighth-grade varsity cross-country team nodded.

"Pay attention," called Carson Krebs.

I have to tell you, this all seemed sort of wrong to me. I mean, cricket? On the Longfellow Middle School football field?

Cricket?

With eighth graders?

With Carson Krebs, who sounded like he'd played cricket forever?

With Coach Krosoczka, who had never played cricket before in his life—obviously—but who suddenly seemed to think cricket was all-fired important—because I guess that's what PE coaches think about every game with a ball.

"Young Master Carter, you are paying attention?"

I nodded—even though I thought I heard the high screeches again. Even the sound of waterfalls, and the hunting calls of hungry dinosaurs, and the slithering of snakes in low grass, and the scrambling of little crocodiles through the underbrush.

⚬ 11 ⚬

AN INNINGS

During a one-day match, each team will have a single innings to bat, limited by the number of overs bowled—an over being six deliveries by the bowler.

WHAT HAPPENED NEXT was sort of what happens in a dream, where you're not sure what anything means, but you figure it all should mean something, but you have no idea what it's supposed to mean, so you're hoping you wake up quickly. The Butler came running toward me—and it was sort of surprising how fast he was coming, because, you may remember, he's sort of big around the belly. Then his arm went over his head, and he threw the ball, and it hit the ground, bounced up, came under my bat that still didn't really feel like a bat but which I was holding straight, I think, and hit the wicket behind me so that the bails flew all over the place.

"Young Master Carter," said the Butler, "your principal task at this moment is to protect your wicket."

"Yeah," said Coach Krosoczka.

"To the death," hollered Billy Colt.

"This means that you are to bat the ball away from it," said the Butler.

"Away from it," said Coach Krosoczka.

"The ball hit the ground," I said.

"As promised," said the Butler.

"So it was, like, a ball or something."

The Butler looked at me. "It *is* a ball," he said.

"No, I mean like the opposite of a strike. A ball."

"You are confusing your sports, young Master Carter. This is cricket."

"Cricket, not baseball," said Coach Krosoczka.

"So the ball is supposed to hit the ground?"

"Of course. Shall we try it again? Coach Krosoczka, if you will toss the ball back and reset the bails. Excellent. Young Master Carter, we are calling that first disaster a trial run. Now, are you ready?"

"Pay attention, Jones," said Carson Krebs.

The sounds of high screeching.

"Mr. Bowles-Fitzpatrick, is the ball going to hit the ground again?"

"With precision and elegance," said the Butler.

"And it's supposed to?"

The Butler looked for a moment as if he were in pain. "Is there a need for excessive repetition?" he said.

I swung the bat a couple of times. "Okay," I said. "Okay, I get it. Let's see that ball."

I did. Three more times. Once under my bat. Once over my bat. And once—and I am not making this up—around my bat. And every time, bails sent flying.

"That last ball was a googly," said the Butler. "Perhaps it was unfair to introduce it at this point."

"Maybe," I said.

"Your bat must be straight when striking the ball."

I made my bat straight.

"And perhaps your knees slightly more bent. You should be ready to react quickly to the ball as it comes to you."

I made my knees slightly more bent.

"Watch the ball into the bat."

I nodded.

"Into the bat," said Coach Krosoczka.

Nodded again.

"Into the bat," said Carson Krebs.

Nodded again.

"So, once more into the breach," said the Butler, and he came running at me with his hand looping over his head, and the ball sped out of his hand and it hit the ground and bounced and I kept my bat straight and my knees slightly more bent so I was ready to react quickly to the ball as it came to me and I watched the ball into the bat and I swung—and you know what?

You know what?

I missed.

"If you would throw it right, I could hit it," I said.

"Young Master Carter, since there are references to cricket in England in the mid-sixteenth century—that is, when the largest English settlements on your American shores comprised two or three fishing hovels leaning together— I believe I may have the advantage over you in terms of understanding how my bowling is judged to be 'right.'"

You see how sometimes the Butler could be a pain in the glutes?

"Shall we see if young Master Krebs still has the knack of it?" said the Butler. "Do you mind, Mr. Barkus?"

Barkus, who had watched this whole disaster, did not mind.

Carson Krebs helped me take the pads off and he put them on. I handed him the bat. He took it like he knew what he was doing.

"Young Master Carter, if you would take young Master Krebs's position in the field as slip. Thank you."

"Yeah," said Coach Krosoczka.

Krebs stood at the wicket. He took a couple of practice swings. When he swung the bat, his forearm was straight and his knees slightly bent.

"You are ready, then?" said the Butler.

Krebs nodded.

The Butler came running at Krebs, and Krebs waited, watched, and the ball came at him and bounced, and Krebs . . .

Well, Krebs batted the ball way over the heads of all the slips.

Actually, he batted the ball way over the heads of all the fielders from the eighth-grade varsity cross-country team and Billy Colt and me every single time he swung.

Did you get that?

Every time he swung.

Even against the googly.

"Well played, young Master Krebs. Balancing off the back foot and quite upright in your stance. One might almost think you had learned from Sachin Tendulkar himself."

Krebs grinned. "I saw him play once. He gave me his bat after the match."

"A noble gesture indeed! Thus the advantage of two years' living in New Delhi. Perhaps you will be so good as to show young Master Barkus the proper hold on the bat, and we will proceed."

I guess you can figure out that the eighth-grade varsity cross-country team had a pretty late practice that morning. You might have thought that Coach Krosoczka was steamed about this, but he wasn't. After Carson Krebs, he was the best batter by far. And when my turn came again, he even gave me a tip that worked out pretty well. "Keep your hands a little lower," he said—and it worked. Not against the googly, but I hit four in a row out from the wicket.

"Not bad," said Coach Krosoczka.

"You're getting your eye in," said Krebs.

"What?" I said.

"You paid attention."

The Butler smiled.

Me too.

The next Saturday morning, we were all back on the pitch—me, Billy Colt, Coach Krosoczka, and every single member of the eighth-grade varsity cross-country team—whose practice on Saturday was now an hour earlier so they could take cricket practice after they ran, and we could be off the field before Vice Principal DelBanco got on to holler at his football players when they screwed up.

This time, we all tried bowling, and it turned out Billy wasn't half bad—or as the Butler said, "You have a promising career ahead, young Master William." He even trapped Carson Krebs leg before wicket. No kidding. And by the end of the morning, he even bowled a googly.

"Did you see that, young Master Carter?" said the Butler. "He pitched on leg stump, but did you follow what happened next?"

I shrugged.

"It was splendid," said the Butler. "Splendid. It turned

to off stump as sharply as you might wish. Absolutely splendid."

"Splendid," I said.

Simon Singh had the longest hits after Krebs, but he got caught in the deep twice. "Bad luck," said the Butler. "But I would put you up first on any team." Which he did when he divided us up and had us try a match, even though there weren't quite enough of us to make up two sides. The Butler bowled and Coach Krosoczka was wicketkeeper for both teams. Simon Singh captained the red team, Carson Krebs the blue—and Krebs put me as opener. He was keystone. We scored twenty-seven runs—and not to brag or anything, but I scored three of them. And even though the red side won because the Butler bowled some that skipped below our bats and he even bowled a yorker once, we all said it was a splendid match.

Really. We all said that.

And you know how good scoring three runs feels when you're playing with a team of eighth graders?

So when the Butler told me that night that he was taking Annie and me to a J. M. W. Turner exhibition at the Marysville Public Library while my mother rested—"a rare and wonderful opportunity"—I didn't say a thing. Not one complaint. Not one.

Not after three runs.

And not after the Butler let me drive the Eggplant to the library.

And not even after we got there and Annie rolled her eyes at how many paintings we were going to have to look at, and I said, "It's a rare and wonderful opportunity," and she hit me.

I never complained. And you know, it really wasn't so bad — for an art exhibition. I mean, there were a lot of ships, and a lot of landscapes, and a lot more ships, and a lot more landscapes, and Annie rolled her eyes a bunch more times, and by the end she was yawning kind of at everything.

But you know what? All these paintings had these skies with swirling clouds that sort of streamed along like they were in high winds, and the winds seemed to push the paint around, like it might all come right out of the pictures and onto the frames. It kind of gave me chills. And there was one painting with an old ship being towed away, and somehow, it made me so sad, sad enough to hold the green marble in my pocket really tight.

The Butler asked how I liked the Turners.

"He doesn't look like he's following the rules," I said.

The Butler nodded.

I looked again at the picture of the ship being towed out.

"And like he . . ."

"Yes?" said the Butler.

"He wants to tell us . . ."

A long moment.

"He wants to tell us that everything has to leave us, sometime or other."

The Butler nodded again. "We are all mortal, and that is the way of it," he said.

I looked at him. "Yeah," I said.

I held the green marble really, really tight.

Anyway, the art exhibit was a lot better—a whole lot better—than Sunday night, when the Butler announced that funds had been set aside in my grandfather's bequest for an education in the arts, and so he was taking me and Emily and Charlie to a ballet exhibition in the brand-new Marysville Civic Auditorium, and so we went, and I won't even tell you what people did up on their toes, on the stage, right in front of everybody. And I won't even tell you what they were wearing.

I *especially* won't tell you what they were wearing—which wasn't much.

Emily and Charlie loved it, and they hugged the Butler and then me when it was finally over.

"Can we go again sometime?" said Charlie.

"Certainly," said the Butler.

"I think Mom would really enjoy a turn," I said.

"That may be," said the Butler.

• 12 •

A GOOGLY

A googly is a deceptive pitch spun with the wrist, so that it seems as though it must angle one way, when in fact it unexpectedly angles exactly the opposite way.

ON MONDAY MORNING, Krebs was waiting for me in the middle school lobby. No kidding. Carson Krebs.

That's Carson Krebs, you remember, who hasn't talked to a sixth grader since he was a sixth grader.

"Hey, Jones," he said.

I looked around. There had to be someone else named Jones.

"Listen, I got an idea on Saturday and I want you to talk to Coach about it."

"Coach Krosoczka?"

He looked at me like I was a stupid sixth grader.

"Bowles-Fitzpatrick. I think he should coach our cricket team."

"He's a butler," I said.

Carson Krebs waited.

"Okay," I said.

"There's a sign-up sheet in the gym. Krosoczka said he'd clear it with the administration and Bowles-Fitzpatrick would be the unofficial but kind of official assistant coach. The team's open to eighth graders and anyone else by invitation. So go look at it — then talk to Coach tonight. I'll talk to him too. Okay?"

"Okay," I said.

He started away, and then turned and called across the lobby. "And Jones!"

"Yeah," I said.

"Remember: This is cricket. This is serious."

I felt myself shiver.

On the way to the gym I saw Singh and Yang and Hopewell and Briggs and Chall and Barkus, and every single one stopped and kind of hit me on the shoulder and asked if I'd seen Krebs yet and wasn't it great and I should go see the sign-up sheet, so by the time I reached the gym my shoulder was sort of sore — but it didn't matter once I got there. Here's what it said on the sign-up sheet:

Eighth-Grade Varsity Cricket Team
Open to All Eighth Graders
Others by Invitation Only

So guess whose name was under "by Invitation Only"?

Mine. And Billy Colt's. We were the only sixth graders on the team. I mean, *invited* on the team.

I saw Billy Colt in homeroom, and while Mrs. Harknet droned, he leaned over and said, "Are you going to do it?"

"Side in," I said.

I guess you can figure out what the rest of the day was like. I mean, how often does a sixth grader get invited onto an eighth-grade team? Never. And we heard about it in every class.

In Language Arts, Mrs. Harknet said she was proud of us for expanding our repertoire beyond typically American sports. (We had to look up *repertoire*, which I think she meant for us to do. You know what language arts teachers are like.) In PE, Coach Krosoczka pretended to be a bowler and bowled a googly, and Billy Colt and I pretended to be batsmen belting it out past the covers—but none of the other sixth graders knew what we were doing. In Math Skills, Mr. Barkus—who I think was pretty proud of his son the cricketer—wondered if he could use the scoring in a cricket match to make up word problems. I hoped not. In Physical Science, Mrs. Wrubell said she had once attended all five days of a test match between England and Australia—"and I never understood a single thing that was going on." Mr. Solaski said he had once seen a test match too. "I left after ten minutes."

But Principal Swieteck was excited. "My husband and I

lived in England for two years while he was studying art," she said. "He played cricket every chance he could. I'm so glad you brought the sport to Longfellow." Then she said, "You didn't really pound stakes into the football field, did you? No, don't say anything. I don't want to know if you did." She looked at me. "Vice Principal DelBanco especially shouldn't know if you did."

That's how it was all day. Billy Colt and I were sixth graders on an eighth-grade team—sort of like Olympic gods.

Can you believe it?

I mean, it was so perfect, I didn't even mind when the Butler told me we were going with Annie to her robotics club open house—my mother, the Butler said, might join us if she was able. But I guess she wasn't able, even though the open house lasted a full hour and a half after school—right through the reruns of *Ace Robotroid and the Robotroid Rangers*—because she never showed. She would probably have been bored anyway. It was an open house with mostly little robots that moved forward three feet and stopped, and little robots that lifted boxes up in the air until the boxes fell from their little claws (or until the boxes made the little robots tip over), and little robots that waved their arms like they were directing a plane into its gate. But I clapped every time Annie's robot made any sign of moving at all: a tread that inched forward, an arm that twitched, a head that turned, a light that flashed for half a second—anything. I didn't mind. That's how perfect my day was.

And when Annie said, "Thanks for coming, Carter," I said, "Anytime," and she said, "Really?" and I said, "Sure," and I meant it.

When we got home that afternoon, Annie went to tell Emily and Charlie about her open house, and I went to find my mother because I was going to need some white pants and a white sweater and some other white stuff, even though we probably couldn't afford it, but I thought I'd ask anyway. I walked through the kitchen and she wasn't there, and then I walked down to the basement to see if she was doing laundry and she wasn't, and then I walked upstairs and the door to her room was closed. I knocked and opened it. She was sitting on the side of the bed.

She was holding Currier's teddy bear.

His name was Ba-Bear.

She was holding Ba-Bear.

"Carter," she said.

That's all. Just "Carter."

I wish I could have said something. But it's not like a play. It's not like someone has written you a bunch of lines and you can just say the right stuff.

I couldn't say anything because I didn't know what to say.

But I could see, all right.

That terrible, terrible day. Cold and wet. Putting Currier in —

"It's your father," she said. "I got an email."

Then I saw something else.

I could see a thousand things at once.

My father transferred back to Afghanistan, and him not telling us because we'd worry it was too dangerous.

My father unconscious, the debris of an explosion still falling around him.

My father lying alongside a road, covered with sand and stone and blood, holding his leg, his men screaming, "Medic! Medic!"

My father in a ditch, shot, someone working over him with bandages, him grimacing.

My father getting carried out in a stretcher, his face grayer than dirt.

My father in a . . .

"Carter," said my mother, and she held out her arms. I sat next to her on the bed and she held me close to her.

I froze.

"Is he all right?" I said.

She held me another minute. Then she sat back. She wiped her eyes. She looked at me. "Carter," she said.

"Mom, is he coming back?" I could barely squeak it out.

And she shook her head.

I saw it again. My father getting carried out on a stretcher. His face grayer than dirt.

My father in a . . .

My father beneath a flag. The flag folded perfectly at the corners.

My father . . .

"He's staying in Germany," she said.

I looked at her. "They won't fly him home?"

"He says Germany is his home."

"What?"

She started to cry again.

"He's hurt?"

She shook her head.

"He's not hurt?"

Shook her head.

"I don't understand."

My mother held me so tightly. "Carter," she said, still crying.

She showed me the email she had printed out.

And that's when I got it.

That's when I really got it.

It wasn't that Captain Jackson Jones was hurt.

It wasn't that Captain Jackson Jones couldn't come home.

It was that Captain Jackson Jones didn't want to come home.

It was that Captain Jackson Jones had met someone else.

It was that Captain Jackson Jones wanted to stay in Germany.

It was that Captain Jackson Jones didn't want to be with us anymore.

How's that for a googly?

• 13 •

THE STUMPS

The three stakes on which the bails sit are the stumps. They stand at both ends of the pitch. Protected by the batsman, they are the object of the bowler.

MY BROTHER, CURRIER, was small as a bug and fast like one too. He was the only kid in the family who liked to play with marbles, but I played with him anyway, and I always gave him back all the marbles I won, especially the green and blue shooters, because those were his favorites—especially his green shooter. He swam like a drowning dog, so lifeguards at pools watched him half out of their chairs. He laughed easy. He sat on his feet with his legs folded underneath him. He read Captain Underpants books. He and I watched reruns of *Ace Robotroid and the Robotroid Rangers* every Saturday morning together—even though I'd seen them all when I was his age and they were sort of dumb then too. He would not eat yellow M&M's. He would not eat pizza if pepperoni had even come near it. He liked to race Ned down the driveway. He liked to race me down the stairs, but I never let him win.

I wish I had. Once, at least.

Currier died when he was six years old. He would be in third grade now, between Charlie and Emily.

One Sunday, when we came home from St. Michael's, he had a fever. My mother figured it was from running around with the other six-year-olds in Junior Church. "He'll be fine in a day or so." She sent him outside to play with me and Ned.

He didn't play much. Ned beat him down the driveway.

That afternoon, he lost at marbles as usual and said I could keep his favorite green shooter. I'd won it fair and square, he said. Don't ever lose it, he said.

Then he went to bed.

I figured we'd play again the next day and I'd let him win the green shooter back.

But the fever wasn't gone in a day or so.

My mother called my father, who was deployed then too. She told him she needed him to come home. We all needed him to come home. Now.

He said he would leave that day, but we waited and waited, and Currier asked when he was coming, and we told him soon. Before you know it. Any day now. Probably tomorrow.

But he didn't make it home in time.

We haven't been to St. Michael's since. My mother told the ladies on the Committee for Funeral Teas that she wouldn't be coming. She told Father Jarrett she didn't need counseling, thank you very much. And no, she didn't need any literature on the process of grieving. She was learning well enough on her own. And as for their prayers . . .

My father returned to his deployment after ten days home.

For a while, Father Jarrett called a couple of times a week. Then my mother stopped answering the phone. And she didn't even return Father Jarrett's calls. After two months, when my mother told him to stop, he did.

This is how it felt after Currier died: like being hit in the glutes and the stomach and the face all at the same time. Every morning when I woke up, there was this moment when I'd forgotten, except the feeling of being hit in the glutes and the stomach and the face was still there. But sometimes, for a moment, I wouldn't remember why, exactly.

Then I would.

And just so you know, when you carry stuff like this around, you never know what kind of day it's going to be. Sometimes you get through the whole day and you're okay. Sometimes there's this little thing that happens—like you see a yellow M&M, or Ned races down the driveway, or some little kid walks by who's the same age as Currier (who's always going to be the same age), and this kid is carrying a Captain Underpants book, or you see your mother crying her eyes out on the side of her bed holding Ba-Bear—and that's it: the rest of the day you feel like you've been hit in the glutes and the stomach and the face again. And you wonder if that's how it's always going to be.

It probably is.

And now my father had finally sent a stupid email. A stupid email to my mother.

A stupid stupid stupid email.

He'd met someone else.

I wondered if the Butler knew.

• 14 •

SIDE OUT

A side, or team, is said to be out when all but one of its batsmen has batted and been dismissed. The two teams then trade places.

THE BUTLER DID DECIDE to be our coach—when I asked him, he said that Carson Krebs had already proffered the question, and he, following proper pondering, would accept. So the next Saturday, the Butler, splendid in his whites, decided to open cricket practice with a drill to demonstrate his skills. He would be the batsman and we would be bowlers, he said. We would stand behind each other in a line, not far up the pitch, and we would bowl at him, one after the other, as quickly as we could. As hard as we could.

He didn't let a single ball through. Not one. The stumps were never touched, the bails never knocked down. Not even when Carson Krebs and Michael Chall bowled two balls at the same time.

The Butler took both balls on his bat together and lobbed them to the slips.

Pretty amazing.

When Chall said he'd be just as good as batsman, the Butler looked at him sort of sideways. "You have a great deal of experience as a batsman, young Master Chall?" he said.

Chall hesitated.

"Some?" said the Butler.

Chall still hesitating.

"Any at all, then?" said the Butler.

"How hard can it be?" said Chall.

The Butler stood very still.

"I mean, you did it," said Chall, "and you're . . ."

"How do you intend to finish that identification?" said the Butler. "'Old'?"

"Not exactly."

"Portly?"

"What does that mean?" said Chall.

"It means 'satisfied with life.' Line up, gentlemen," said the Butler, and he tossed cricket balls to us all.

Chall did pretty well as batsman. Two balls got through, but they didn't hit the stumps. Then Krebs bowled the seventh ball, and maybe it jumped a bit to the inside stump. Maybe it hit a bump in the turf. Maybe he bowled a googly. But whatever he did, the ball jumped up and Chall didn't move and it took him square in the stomach. Chall coughed and turned a little so that he faced the pitch. He started to double over. And all this happened at the same time that Singh, who was right behind Krebs, bowled his ball, and it bounced into Chall too, but a little lower.

I guess you know what happened then.

And as the rest of the eighth-grade varsity cricket team rushed toward Michael Chall, and then stepped back when he started to gag, and then rushed away when he threw up what had probably been a pretty big breakfast, I thought, *That's how I feel all the time now.* Like a couple of cricket balls have smashed into my stomach.

Except after a while, Chall was better.

At home, we mostly talked around my father, bowling googlies *away* from the stumps. My mother and I didn't say anything about it to the girls. I mean, what could we say? "Hey, Emily, Charlie, Annie, we've got something to tell you. Daddy isn't coming home because now he wants to live in Germany with someone else and not with us."

It isn't exactly news you want to break to your sisters.

Those first nights after the email, my mother decided to cook instead of the Butler, and she clattered around in the kitchen a lot, making everything we liked. Macaroni and cheese with bacon for Emily, fried banana dessert for Charlie, spaghetti and sweet Italian sausage for Annie. They were pretty happy, because they didn't know why she was making macaroni and cheese and fried bananas and spaghetti with sweet Italian sausage.

But I knew.

You know what macaroni and cheese and fried bananas and spaghetti with sweet Italian sausage taste like when your father isn't coming home from deployment because he doesn't want to?

Nothing.

They tasted like nothing.

They may as well have been liverwurst.

Well, not liverwurst.

Boiled ham and green beans.

They may as well have been boiled ham and green beans.

I don't know what they tasted like to my mother, since she mostly didn't eat them. She'd sit at the table and smile as Emily and Charlie and Annie chattered about school. When we were done the Butler would come out from the kitchen and take all the plates, and my mother would get homework organized, and then she'd sit in the living room and read some book without turning a page. The girls would finish homework and they'd come downstairs and turn on the television, and the Butler would come out from the kitchen and turn it to PBS. In an hour or so the Butler would announce bedtimes. Emily and Charlie and Annie would go upstairs and Annie would complain that I got to stay up later than she did, and the Butler would nod and explain that I had more homework in sixth grade and would she prefer staying up for another hour to do some of Mr. Barkus's math problems in which you had to show your work and justify your solutions?

And after all that, my mother would put her book down and she'd go into the kitchen and thank the Butler for all he had done, and then she would go upstairs too. And after a while the Butler would come out and say goodnight, and that I had ten minutes left before bedtime, that preparing my backpack would not be amiss, and to dream imaginatively. Then he'd go home to the Krebses' house.

It was pretty lonely. Like being in the Blue Mountains all by yourself, listening to the slithering in the low grass.

Feeling like two cricket balls had just bounced into me because Captain Jackson Jonathan Jones wasn't coming home.

And there was no one to talk to about it. I mean, my mother didn't want to say anything. And the girls didn't know. And I wasn't going to tell Billy Colt since it would have gotten around the whole school by lunchtime.

I don't think I would even have told Father Jarrett, and it's, like, against the law for him to repeat stuff.

So there was no one to talk to.

You know what?

It really stunk.

You know what else stinks?

Ballet.

Ballet really stinks.

And who knew there was so much of it in Marysville, New York?

So when the Butler asked me to attend a performance of scenes from *Swan Lake* courtesy of my grandfather's endowment in the arts because Emily and Charlie really really really wanted to see it and love of the arts was always to be encouraged, and though he had three tickets he had another commitment that night but he would drive us, and would I be so kind as to chaperone, what was I supposed to say?

Because Emily and Charlie were watching me the whole time the Butler was asking.

What could I do?

That night, there were a whole lot of people running around the stage up on their toes, which is sort of pointless and not the way normal people run, as anyone could tell you — and a whole lot of twirling around, which is another thing that normal people tend not to do — and a whole lot of graceful posing by the girls while the guys held them up in the air, which is still another thing that normal people tend not to do. Who poses gracefully when they're being held up in the air?

Ballet stinks.

But Emily loved it and Charlie loved it and they hugged me when it was finally over.

Later, the Butler asked me how I liked *Swan Lake*.

"It stunk," I said.

"Perhaps, young Master Carter, you might expand upon that judgment."

"It really stunk," I said.

"So I should consider that ballet, as an art form, is dead to you, then?" said the Butler.

"It really, really stunk," I said.

"Dead and buried," he said.

On the last Friday of September, the wind was cool and dry in that way that tells you maybe summer is finally over. It was the kind of day when you notice that some of the trees have changed to yellows and reds, and the breeze has started to take down a few of the leaves, and there are pots of orange and yellow chrysanthemums on porches, and last summer seems a bazillion years ago and next summer's vacation seems a bazillion years away—because it is.

It was that kind of day when Krebs found me before school and told me to hold up. He and the rest of the eighth-grade varsity cross-country team were heading to the locker room, since they ran in the mornings now so they could play cricket in the afternoons.

"How about we stay late after practice and get in some more batting?" he said.

Remember, Carson Krebs is an eighth grader. He never talks to a normal sixth grader. Even to a sixth grader on an eighth-grade team *By Invitation Only*, he hardly ever talks.

"Sure," I said.

"We'll set up a net behind the wicket and take turns batting."

"Sounds good," I said.

"Just for a little while," he said.

"Okay," I said.

"Until the late buses," he said.

"Okay."

That afternoon was great. We stayed late after practice, and I bowled first, and Krebs batted away ball after ball after ball. I came close to his wicket a couple of times, and once I thought I even nicked a stump—but the bails didn't come down.

And once . . .

"Was that a googly?" said Krebs.

I nodded.

"Not bad. Let's see that googly."

But I couldn't make it work again.

Then Krebs bowled, and I batted away most of them. He hit my wicket three times—twice with a googly—and caught two of my shots. He was that good.

Simon Singh came by, and Michael Chall, and Steve Yang, but Krebs told them it was just the two of us practicing, and they said okay. And that's what we did until it was almost time for the late buses, and we took down the net and gathered the cricket balls and carried everything into the gym, and Krebs said, "You're striking the ball really well."

"Not like you," I said.

"So listen, Jones," he said. "Things will get sorted."

"You mean in cricket?"

"In cricket, too."

101

I looked at him.

He opened the door to Coach Krosoczka's office and hauled the bag of cricket balls inside. I followed him in and propped the bats on the bag. Krebs folded the net on top.

"Coach gave you a key?" I said.

"We don't have an equipment manager, so I'm it. For cross and for cricket."

We left. Krebs locked the door behind him and hefted his backpack to his shoulder. "I was a couple of years younger than you when my mother left. I couldn't figure it out. I didn't even know if I should be mad or sad or what. And my dad might just as well have walked out too. He used to be this amazing athlete. Cricket, mostly, but soccer too, and cross-country. He coached our school cricket team in New Delhi for the two years we were there. When she left, he started to spend most of his time up in his room, when he wasn't burning something in the kitchen." He shrugged. "He still spends most of his time up in his room."

"So did things get sorted?"

He shrugged again. "I cook now. We get by. And Coach is working on him."

We headed toward the late buses idling in front of the school. The wind had come up, blustery and even cold, and I was sweaty enough to feel the chill.

"See you tomorrow," said Krebs. "And Jones . . ."

"Yeah?"

"Don't let the bails come down. Okay? Just don't."

And suddenly, I couldn't let him go. It seemed important—like something that really mattered was happening. Something that mattered so much, I could almost have started to bawl.

Something I should pay attention to.

"How do you keep the bails from coming down?" I said.

Krebs started to laugh. "You know what Coach would say. 'Make good decisions and remember who you are.'" Then he ran to the north side bus—it was just about to pull away—and it stopped and the door opened. He waved, and was gone.

The eastbound bus was waiting, and I got on that.

The whole ride home, I wondered how I was going to keep the bails up.

• 15 •

THE SHOOTER

A shooter is a ball from the bowler that, after it bounces, comes in much lower than the batsman had anticipated. The surprising placement can lead to many a fallen bail.

THE BUTLER WAS waiting for me—almost as if he knew I'd be on the late bus. He stood outside the house, Ned beside him on his leash.

"Really?" I said. "I just got home."

"Something Ned is most keenly aware of, as you may conclude by the manner in which his back legs are crossed."

"His back legs aren't crossed."

"Only because they are too short." He handed me the leash. "Shall I accompany you?" he said.

I shrugged.

"Literacy skills are in short supply in your nation, young Master Carter. You would do well not to contribute to the problem."

"I should say hi to my mother first."

"Your mother has an appointment at St. Michael's."

I looked at him.

"She never goes to St. Michael's," I said.

"Then today would represent an exception to the rule. Come along." So we set off around the block, Ned pulling out in front because he was pretty eager. Obviously.

The day had gotten even colder during the bus ride home, and the wind was taking off more of the early yellow leaves and blowing Ned's ears back. He half closed his eyes against it and trotted on.

"You had an extra practice, then?" said the Butler.

"Carson Krebs and me."

"An estimable young man. Living in India for any time at all will make a gentleman of you."

"I suppose," I said. We passed the Ketchums' azaleas, the flowers almost all gone now. The Briggses' rhododendrons, the Rockcastles' holly hedge, the Koertges' petunias—their flowers almost all gone too. When we got to the end of Billy Colt's driveway, we stopped for Ned. "Hey, how did you know about the extra practice?" I said.

"I come from the land of Sir Arthur Conan Doyle," the Butler said. "I deduced."

"No you didn't," I said. "You knew about it."

The Butler, for once, didn't say anything.

"You talked to Krebs."

Still nothing.

"You told him to meet me after school. You told him to set up a practice so...what? So he could talk to me? About my father? You told him about my father? How did you even know?"

"Are you accusing, young Master Carter?"

"Deducing. And accusing."

"Is it your intention to allow Ned to relieve himself against the last of these day lilies?"

"It's where he always does it. Stop stalling."

The Butler waited for a moment. Then he said, slowly, "You will remember, young Master Carter, that I have taken rooms with Mr. Krebs, and—"

"Geez, so you blabbed everything."

The Butler turned to me. "I do not blab, young Master Carter. I inquire, I learn, and I inform."

"You blabbed."

"And the British lament the lack of subtlety and nuance in the American exploitation of our language. How could we have possibly come to that conclusion?"

"You blabbed."

"I hoped to encourage camaraderie during a time when you might feel a tad lost."

"You still blabbed."

"And I hoped to encourage it with a young man who has been in a similar situation. I believed there might be a kind of understanding that would be healthy for you both."

And I don't know why, but as Ned stood there, trying to

figure out which day lily he was going to finish off with, I thought I was going to bawl. Or maybe throw up. Or maybe both.

In the Blue Mountains of Australia, you can walk and walk and never have to think about anything except the trail.

In the Blue Mountains, all you hear is the sound of water dripping and rushing and falling.

Sometimes white birds screeching. Hunting calls, slithering, scrambling.

In the Blue Mountains, I walked with my father for miles, and we never had to talk. When we stopped for lunch, we each knew what to do. When we stopped to make camp, we each knew what to do. Once I almost showed him Currier's green marble, but I didn't. "I wish it could always be like this," he said one dark night while I was trying to see stars between the high leaves of the eucalyptus trees. I went to sleep with him humming Beethoven.

The Butler took Ned's leash. "It's all right, young Master Carter. Things will sort out."

"How?"

He looked at me. "You will learn to sort them."

I wasn't so sure, but I couldn't say that since I was about to bawl.

"Shall we go on home, then?" said the Butler. "Your mother will be back from her appointment."

We did, but when we went up the steps, just before we

went in the back door, I turned to the Butler and said, "You still blabbed."

And the Butler said, "So I did."

It rained on Saturday—more sleet than rain—so there was no cricket practice. It rained on Sunday, too, so according to the Butler, there was nothing for it but to do homework, which Annie, Charlie, and Emily finished in about ten seconds. This, said the Butler, gave Annie the splendid opportunity to spend a trifle more time on her piano scales, to be followed by her rhythmic exercises with the metronome, and he exiled her to the living room for an hour.

For enjoying Annie's exile too much, Charlie and Emily, the Butler said, were to spend that same hour in their room practicing archeology, hoping, he said, to discover the color of the carpet that lay beneath their layers of debris.

"It's blue," said Emily.

The Butler bent down to her. "I challenge you to prove it to me," he said.

And now, I want it to be clear that I didn't say a thing about enjoying Annie's exile.

But it didn't matter.

The Butler stood up. "And so to you, young Master Carter," he said.

"To me?"

He opened my social studies book and turned a few pages. "You are studying the rebellion of the American colonies?"

"The American Revolution," I said. "I have to do a report on the Declaration of Independence."

The Butler sighed. "That does seem a tad dreary."

"No kidding."

"On the other hand—"

You know how writers sometimes say that someone's ears perked up? It was almost like that really happened with the Butler. He smiled and his eyes sort of gleamed, and he said, "Your report might become of interest if you were to articulate the British perspective on that document and its rash call for independence."

I looked at him. "Why would I do that? The British didn't think there was any reason for the Declaration of Independence."

"And how discerning they were," said the Butler.

"What does that mean?"

"It means that there was no justification for such a declaration," said the Butler.

"How about taxation without representation?"

"An irksome thing, no doubt—and one faced annually by the inhabitants of your District of Columbia, which is currently the seat of your American government. And yet you do not see those citizens setting up barricades and seceding."

"So? How many people actually live there? Like, fourteen?"

"Certainly, young Master Carter, you are not seriously arguing that matters of truth and justice should be decided numerically?"

"Okay, how about the Boston Massacre? You think it's okay for a bunch of soldiers to shoot down innocent civilians?"

"Hurting innocent civilians is the purview of terrorists. However, as your own John Adams proved at trial, soldiers defending themselves from a mob in the process of attacking them is hardly shooting down innocent civilians. And John Adams, I hasten to remind you, became your second president, proving that some Americans, at least, may be wise and good men and still rise to power."

"And all the threats by the British government?"

"Did the British government detain American officials and subsequently tar and feather them? Did the British government board British merchantmen and ransack them, throwing their cargo into the harbor? Did the British government attack the home of the governor of Massachusetts, scattering much of the work that was meant to be published as the history of that colony? Did the British government—"

"All right, all right. But I remember who I am, which is an American, and I can't write stuff like that."

"Of course not, young Master Carter, because trying to think objectively in order to discern and express truth is so much less worthy than parroting centuries-old propaganda."

I stared at the Butler. He was winning, and he knew it.

"How about Benedict Arnold?" I said. "Huh? How about him?"

"I am not quite sure how Benedict Arnold represents a

justification of your Declaration of Independence, unless you mean that document to express a rationale for boorish and illegal behavior—which of course it does. However, in the cause of objectivity, I note that the patriot Benedict Arnold, having been scorned for extraordinary acts of valor by your Congress, chose for a representative pittance to turn over an American stronghold to rightful hands for the noble purpose of ending a war ruinous to two countries, though he understood the calamitous consequences to his personal safety and estate. Is this the gentleman to whom you refer?"

I looked at the Butler. "Remember how you blabbed the other day?"

The Butler looked at me. "Young Master Carter, might I suggest that you work to overcome the bias of your position and begin with words to this effect: 'Due to the madness of the times' or 'The revolutionaries, in their arrogance' or 'Ignoring the many kindnesses of their mother country in their headlong ambition.' I suspect any of those will do."

"And those aren't biased at all," I said.

"Let me brew some tea to inspire you," the Butler said. "That is, unless you wish to emulate your ancestors and throw all the Earl Grey into the swimming pool next door."

"Blabber," I said.

The Butler went into the kitchen to brew the tea. He walked through the living room first, though, and asked Annie if she might pause in her scales and play "Rule Britannia!" please. *Fortissimo.*

• 16 •

A DRY WICKET

If the pitch has become worn, with loss of grass, it may be said to be a dry wicket. This surface usually allows for faster bowling, but it also benefits the batsman, in that the bounce is truer and spins are less effective. A wicket that is especially dry, however, may develop cracks that can be particularly useful to a clever spinner.

ONE MORNING in the Blue Mountains of Australia, I woke up before my father. I tried to get the fire started so I could maybe cook breakfast, but I could hardly get it going since the wood was so wet. I had to wait until he got up. He mumbled something and then he got it started like the wood was dry as could be, because that's what someone who's put in his time in the U.S. Army can do. He cooked bacon and powdered scrambled eggs and we ate them, and we didn't talk much. We listened to the screeching birds overhead, and the water everywhere, and the wind in the high eucalyptus branches. Then we got all the stuff together. My father loaded most of it into his backpack.

That was our last morning in the Blue Mountains. I

remember the air got the bluest it had ever been that afternoon, when we were climbing out. And then we got in the Jeep and drove back to the city.

I cried.

We still hadn't told the girls.

I almost did the next Saturday afternoon. I almost did. I was standing with the Butler and watching Charlie at her soccer match, cheering her on as she ran up and down the field. Sometimes she kicked at a ball that was flying past her, but she never touched it. She mostly talked to one of the girls from Ellenville Elementary until they both just sat down and pulled at the grass.

When she came off the field, she asked, "Did we win?" and I hugged her hard.

On Sunday morning, the Butler and I took Emily out to breakfast because she had spent Saturday afternoon not at a soccer game but with the dentist, who had filled a cavity. So she wanted something special too now, and the Butler said we would go to a nice restaurant where they did not serve Ace Robotroid Sugar Stars, and Emily said she wanted Mom to come with us, but the Butler explained that she wasn't feeling quite up to that and we should go along to leave the house quiet for her. So we went — I drove the Eggplant, by the way — and the Butler ordered steel-cut oatmeal with whole milk for all of us — "Shall we splurge and have cranberries on top?"

113

he said—but after he ordered I said I had to go to the bathroom, and I found our waiter and asked if he could put Ace Robotroid Sugar Stars on top instead of cranberries. "Of course," he said. And that's what he did.

Emily squealed when she saw them. It had been a while.

"You have defiled the oatmeal," said the Butler to the waiter.

"Orders are orders, bud," said the waiter. He nodded at me.

Emily got up and hugged me. "You are my favorite brother," she said. "Can you be my Favorite Person of the Week in school?"

I hugged her back.

The Butler did not leave a tip.

In the afternoon, we all drove to Spicers U-Pick Apples. I drove again, sitting on a cushion to give me greater height: "We would rather not attract the attention of uniformed officers who may not look kindly upon your automotive skills," said the Butler. My mother sat in the back, pretty stiff, holding Annie, Emily, and Charlie with a death grip.

"Mr. Spicer," said the Butler, "seems to be troubled by both a deleted apostrophe and an infelicitous abbreviation."

"What's *infelicitous*?" said Emily.

"The noxious result of not attending to one's grammar," said the Butler, "which, of course, will afflict no one in this automobile."

We picked three bushels of apples, and then Emily and Charlie decided that picking bushels of apples was boring. The apple stand was selling Dreamsicles and they didn't cost all that much, and the two of them had already helped pick three bushels of apples, so couldn't they . . .

I went with Annie and Emily and Charlie to buy Dreamsicles, and after they'd finished getting orange hands and orange lips and—for Emily and Charlie—orange shirts, I helped the Butler carry the three bushels to the Eggplant.

The Butler drove home. He said the girls could sit up with him after a proper washing of hands and face—which they did in the water fountain—and then they squeezed into the front seat and he wrapped the seat belt around all three of them.

"That's probably illegal," I said.

"I have met the principal of Longfellow Middle School," said the Butler.

"How's that going to help?"

"One never knows how one's associations may prove invaluable at unexpected moments," said the Butler.

I sat in the back and my mother took my hand.

Her hand was cold.

"Do you remember the last time we picked apples?" she whispered.

I nodded.

"Remember how Currier . . ." That's all she said. That's all she *could* say.

We drove home holding hands, and the green marble was in my pocket, and all I could think about—all *we* could think about—was Currier biting into an apple one fall day not so long ago, and him finding a worm and spitting it out, and then holding up the apple in one hand and the worm in the other, laughing, the rest of us wanting to throw up.

"I bet *you* couldn't find a worm, Carter," he said.

"You win," I said, and he laughed and laughed and laughed.

Monday morning, I told my mother I was going to articulate the British perspective on the Declaration of Independence.

"Really?" she said.

"Yup," I said.

"What are you going to say?"

"That the Declaration of Independence was a marketing scam."

A long pause. "A marketing scam?"

"Yup," I said.

"Do you think Mr. Solaski will be okay about this?"

"It's his assignment," I said.

"How do you think everyone else in the class will react?"

"They'll figure out I'm trying to think objectively in order to discern and express truth instead of parroting centuries-old propaganda," I said.

116

My mother looked at me. "Sure they will," she said.

Annie and Charlie and Emily and I got in the Eggplant to drive to school. Emily could hardly wait to get there because she was going on a field trip to the Marysville Fire Station.

"That will be splendid," said the Butler.

Charlie was giving a report on E. Nesbit, who was now her favorite author in the whole world.

"Proving," said the Butler, "that we are all capable of growing into discerning readers."

Annie was trying out for the fifth-grade girls' football team during her gym class.

"You mean soccer team," I said.

"Football," she said. Then she smiled at the Butler, who smiled back in the rearview mirror.

"Exactly right," he said. "And young Master Carter, what does this day hold for you?"

"I'm about to tell my class that we shouldn't have become independent."

"Quite right," said the Butler. "Think of the advantages if you had remained a colony and never taken up rebellion."

"Like what?"

"You would not only have learned how to speak the language properly—as, for example, the avoidance of abrupt and inelegant sentence fragments—but you would have discovered the glories of cooperation while at the same time becoming aware of the calming properties of a good tea."

"Probably they didn't care too much about tea while they were fighting the American Revolution."

"Perhaps in a rebellion, that would be so," said the Butler. "In the midst of great anxiety and great sadness, it takes an honorable man to nourish the goodness around him, small and fragile as it may seem."

"Is that one of those things you say that's supposed to mean a whole lot more than it seems to mean at first?"

"It is one of those things that a lifetime of reading Dickens and Trollope would annotate. But given the literary limitations of an American curriculum, we should be heartened that experience and the wisdom that comes from it—as well as an adherence to decorum—are good tutors."

I looked at the Butler. "That still sounds like you're trying to convert me into a gentleman."

"Thank you," said the Butler.

And that's how I went to school that day: wondering what was so good about stupid adherence to stupid decorum.

By the way, I'd stopped watching for an email from my father. I guess I knew it wasn't coming.

Probably he didn't know what stupid decorum was either.

· 17 ·

LEG BEFORE WICKET

If a batsman prevents a bowled ball from striking the wicket by placing his leg or body in its path to block it, the umpire may dismiss the batsman for being leg before wicket.

HERE'S WHAT HAPPENED after I finished my oral report on the Declaration of Independence and the American Rebellion.

Mr. Solaski gave a long, low whistle. "Well," he said, "it's usually valuable to hear alternate viewpoints."

Patty Trowbridge raised her hand and asked what the patriots used to do to Tory traitors.

Ryan Moore turned to me. "They tarred and feathered them," he said.

Actually, he didn't say, "They tarred and feathered them." He snarled it.

Billy Colt looked at me and shook his head. "Nice knowing you," he whispered.

It was a long class.

When Patty Trowbridge began her report on Betsy Ross, she said that her ancestors had fought and died for our freedom at Bunker Hill—"unlike some."

When Jennifer Washburn began her report on the battle at the Old North Bridge, she said she had a relative who'd helped to smuggle Abraham Lincoln into Washington for his inauguration—"unlike some."

And when Ryan Moore began his report on the Boston Massacre, he said he was glad true Americans like Crispus Attucks had stood up—"unlike some."

"It's not a big deal," I said to Billy Colt at noon in the cafeteria. He was opening my lunch to see what the Butler had packed. "I mean, it all happened a bazillion years ago."

"Do you want these raisin scones?" he said.

"And they're all dead."

"Or maybe they're blueberry."

Ryan Moore stopped at our table.

I looked at him.

"Tory traitor," he said. He took the two scones and walked away.

Billy Colt took out the hard-boiled eggs.

"So can I have these?" he said.

The Butler picked us up in the Eggplant. Annie and Charlie and Emily talked fast, like they had eaten too much sugar.

Annie said she scored three goals during football tryouts and it would have been four if she hadn't been fouled at the last minute, and she got a 99 percent on her spelling and it would have been 100 percent except she forgot a period on one of her sentences, and Coach Krosoczka said during football tryouts that she had a very natural throw-in. Charlie got to read the Pledge of Allegiance over the PA during morning announcements and Principal Swieteck said she had done so well that she could lead the school in the Pledge of Allegiance the whole week, and everyone loved her report on E. Nesbit except the boys but who cared what they thought? And Emily said the Marysville Fire Station was wonderful and they had blown the sirens and everything, and she'd asked if she could slide down the pole but they said they only let firefighters do that and maybe someday she'd be a firefighter and she could slide down the pole all she wanted. And then later back at school everyone had gotten a new set of crayons and it wasn't the usual sixteen pack, it was a sixty-four pack, and it had gold and silver and bronze and everything.

"And how was your day, young Master Carter?" said the Butler.

"Great," I said.

"Your inflection suggests otherwise," he said.

"Well, since I got called a Tory traitor, maybe it wasn't so great."

The Butler looked at me in the rearview mirror.

"And of course you pointed out to your misinformed peers

that it would be impossible for an American to be a member of a British political party."

"Yup. That's exactly what I told them."

A whole minute went by.

"And aquamarine," said Emily.

"You understand, young Master Carter, that disagreement need not be unpleasant," said the Butler.

"It is in sixth grade."

"The patterns you set in—"

"Mr. Bowles-Fitzpatrick, I really don't need to hear this right now."

We drove the rest of the way home without talking, except for Charlie, who said, "Why is everyone mad?" It was misting out, and the wipers went back and forth.

"Angry," said the Butler. "'Mad' refers to the ailment rather than the emotion."

"Oh," said Charlie.

"And cherry red," said Emily.

I didn't say anything.

I was mad.

On that morning in the Blue Mountains of Australia when I woke up before my father, I really wanted to get the fire started so I could cook breakfast. It wasn't raining, exactly, but everything was sopping wet—not just on the ground, but up through the whole forest. The trees were black with the damp, and the ground soft enough that if you pressed your sneaker into it, water came up. Dripping from every branch. Beads of water dripping off our tent. The sound of dripping almost as loud as the white stream that was running high—or maybe it was always that high—down a bank by where we were camped. If I had wanted to wake my father up, I would have had to shout over all the dripping and streaming and squishing and gurgling.

The wood we had stacked the night before was sopping, like it needed to be wrung out. I poked around in the ashes from last night's campfire, but all that was left were two pathetic embers winking in and out in all that dampness. They didn't have much longer to live, and laying sopping wood on them wasn't going to save them. So I left the campsite and went into the high grass to snap some small dead branches off the trees, since maybe they wouldn't be as wet as everything else. And they weren't. I got a couple of handfuls, and then a few more, and then I took off my T-shirt and loaded them all into it, since my shirt was already sopping wet from the water coming off the branches and it wasn't doing me much good anyway. On the way back, every big leaf—and there were plenty of them—angled itself to dump cold water down my back and into my jeans and down to my sneakers.

I brought the branches that were at least drier back to camp. One of the embers hadn't made it, but the other was still fighting. I picked out the thinnest and driest branches and laid them crosswise over the fighting ember, and I began to blow as gently as I could. The ember began to flare a bright yellow, and a few quick sparks shot into the branches.

I thought there might even have been a little smoke coming up.

I blew gently again.

The ember sputtered.

I blew some more.

A flame steadied into a pale yellow.

More blowing.

A snap, then another, and two of the twigs showed flame. Then more quick snaps, some sparks, and two more twigs burning.

That's when I noticed my father was standing there. Completely dry. As if a drip wouldn't dare come near him.

"We're not going to be able to do much with that," he said.

He knelt down beside me and swiped all the twigs away. Then he started to build the fire all over again.

We didn't talk. I mostly listened to the screeching birds overhead, and the water everywhere, and the wind in the high eucalyptus branches.

The night after my report on the Declaration of Independence, my mother was over at St. Michael's again. "Father Jarrett has asked her to attend to certain budget matters for the next calendar year," said the Butler.

"That doesn't start for almost three months," I said.

"Then there is no time to lose. Is there anything I might do to help with homework?"

"I only have social studies," I said.

"Then perhaps . . ."

"You helped me enough in social studies."

"Young Master Carter, I suggested new ideas for you to consider—and clearly, they were new ideas for much of your class to consider as well."

"It's not like they really considered them," I said.

"And so you face a curious dilemma, one you will face often if you choose to live a life of integrity and challenge. Is it better to consider all ideas, to determine which one seems to you most reasonable and worthy, and then to speak your mind? Or is it better to follow old patterns and to acquiesce quietly into a general conformity?"

"What does 'acquiesce quietly into a general conformity' even mean?"

"I believe you know," said the Butler.

I looked at him. "I think that's the one I want."

"No, it is not," said the Butler. "That is the one that someone stuck in middle school would choose."

"I *am* stuck in middle school."

"You are attending middle school, young Master Carter. You need not be stuck there."

"That feels like a googly," I said.

"Not at all. These are straight bowls. All you have to do is to swing your bat."

"My father isn't coming home."

I don't know why I said that to the Butler. It just came out. I don't know why it just came out. But it did.

I really don't know why I said that.

The Butler looked at me, then looked away, then looked back at me. "Young Master Carter," he said. Almost whispered. He tried again. "Young Master Carter, I—"

"He's not coming home. He wants to live in Germany."

A long time went by.

"Maybe it's because of us."

Another long time.

"Not exactly a straight bowl," I said.

"No," said the Butler. "Not a straight bowl at all."

"So how do I sort that out?"

"By making good decisions and remembering who you are."

"Like keeping the bails up?"

"Exactly like. None of this is your doing, young Master Carter."

Another long time. There were a lot of long times.

"How can I be sure?" I said.

"Because, Carter," said the Butler, "I am telling you it is so. And I have something for you."

He went downstairs, came back, and handed me a book: *The Complete Sherlock Holmes* by Sir Arthur Conan Doyle.

"I saw the movies," I said.

"Which means that you have yet to learn anything at all about Sir Arthur's conception of the great detective. I suggest beginning with 'The Adventure of the Speckled Band.' Please note its insistence that experience and wisdom and adherence to decorum will have their way."

"I don't know what that means either."

"I think you do," said the Butler. "As a matter of fact, I wonder if you know it better than you imagine."

I looked at the Butler, and I began to hope that maybe Krebs and the Butler were right. Maybe some things could get sorted.

But I still didn't know how.

° 18 °

RUNNING BETWEEN THE WICKETS

Runs are scored as the batsmen sprint from their wickets, carrying their bats and placing them or some part of the body into the crease in front of the opposite wicket. In this manner, the batsman facing the bowler will continue to bat and accumulate runs until he is dismissed.

FOR THE NEXT three days in school, I tried to keep the bails up.

It's not easy being a Tory—which everyone should know is impossible for an American to be. But apparently the news hadn't reached the sixth grade of Longfellow Middle School.

I mean, how would you like it if when you stood up to recite the Pledge of Allegiance, Patty Trowbridge asked Mrs. Harknet if someone who didn't believe in the Declaration of Independence should be allowed to stand up and pledge allegiance?

How would you like it?

So you know what? It was kind of sweet to be up in front of Emily's class and listen to her introduce me as "My

Favorite Person of the Week," and then have a bunch of second graders ask how old I was, what TV show did I like—I told them I liked *Ace Robotroid and the Robotroid Rangers* because . . . just because—what did I want to be when I grew up, did I ever meet anyone famous, did I know that Sarah Bixby thought I was cute—which sort of ended the questions because Sarah Bixby turned red and ran out of the room and Emily's teacher had to go after her.

It was kind of nice to be Emily's Favorite Person of the Week.

I never would have thought so, but it really was.

It was already mid-October, and the trees had shaken down most of their leaves, and there weren't going to be too many more cricket practices. The Butler said we should try to get in at least one match, even though we didn't have enough for two full teams, so it wouldn't exactly be an authentic match. He scheduled it for the last Saturday in October, early in the morning since the Longfellow Middle School Minutemen were playing their football game at ten o'clock.

Krebs would be the captain of Team India. Singh would be captain of Team Britannia. And even though the Butler kept saying, "All good fun, boys," Krebs had never lost anything in his life, and Singh said Team Britannia would teach him the agony of defeat, and Krebs started to walk around the school with Sachin Tendulkar's bat, and Singh's mother handed out Team Britannia sweatshirts with British flags on the back and lions rampant on the front. I mean, really. Lions rampant?

And just for the record, no one in the whole sixth grade called Singh or anyone on Team Britannia a Tory—maybe because it's smart for a sixth grader not to call an eighth grader anything but an eighth grader.

The day Team Britannia wore their sweatshirts to school, Krebs told everyone on Team India to give him their Longfellow Middle School hoodies the next morning. We all did. The day after that, he gave them back to us, and printed across the backs were names like these:

Sachin Tendulkar

Sunil Gavaskar

Kapil Dev

Anil Kumble

Virender Sehwag

Krebs was Sachun Tendulkar. I was Virender Sehwag.

"Who's Virender Sehwag?" I said.

Krebs looked at me like I was a stupid sixth grader. "The year 2004? India versus Pakistan? The first player from India to score over three hundred? Anil Kumble at spinner?"

"Oh yeah," I said. "I remember. The year 2004. I think I was almost conceived by then."

Krebs laughed. "Okay. I guess it's different if you've lived in New Delhi."

"Maybe a little bit."

"But at least I didn't announce to everyone that I was against the American Revolution."

"I'm not against the American Revolution."

"Benedict Arnold was a good guy?"

There was no use explaining. So I put on my hoodie and the rest of Team India put on theirs and we went out to practice our batting. And even though Sachin Tendulkar hit something like thirty-five runs, Virender Sehwag didn't do so bad that afternoon either.

He kept the bails up.

When I got home, I walked Ned around the block with my mother, who had never before walked Ned around the block. Never once. The Ketchums' azaleas had lost all their flowers. The Briggses' rhododendrons were putting on their darker green for winter. The Rockcastles' holly hedge was filled with red berries. And the Koertges' petunias were all dead. My mother bent down to touch the last brown leaves.

"Do you remember in 2004 when Virender Sehwag scored over three hundred runs in one test match?" I said.

My mother looked at me like I was speaking in hieroglyphics. "Should I remember that?"

"He was the first Indian player to do it. Score three hundred runs. In one test match."

We kept walking until Ned stopped by Billy Colt's driveway.

"I'm sure Mr. Sehwag must have been very happy."

"India beat Pakistan, so I guess his whole team was happy."

"Good for them," said my mother.

I don't think she really cared.

"Carter," she said.

Ned finished up. I saw Billy Colt looking out his window, and I waved. He was on Team Britannia, so I was glad Ned did what he did where he did it, which he would have done even if Billy Colt was on Team India, but somehow now it felt right.

"Carter," said my mother, "how are you feeling about . . ."

Ned pulled on his lead. He was ready to move on.

"About . . ."

"Okay," I said.

We got to the day lilies on the other side of the driveway. Ned took care of them. For a little dachshund, it was really amazing how many day lilies he could take care of.

"Okay," my mother said.

"Are you glad the Butler's here?" I asked.

She nodded. "Paul came at the right time, didn't he?"

She called him Paul. Really. Paul.

"We could have used him during the other deployments," she said.

I nodded.

"It was like he knew when we needed him most," she said.

I looked at her.

"When we needed him most," I said.

She nodded. "Does Ned always do that to the day lilies?"

I had just figured something out.

That night, after supper, I dried dishes for the Butler. It was the only time he ever had his jacket off—except for cricket. The sleeves of his white shirt were rolled up, his cuff links on the windowsill. His vest was still buttoned tightly, and his tie was, as usual, perfect.

"Do you always wear a vest?" I said.

"Waistcoat," he said. "And yes."

"You know who Virender Sehwag is?" I asked.

"Do I know who Virender Sehwag is?" said the Butler. "That, young Master Carter, is akin to asking if I know who Donald Bradman is."

I finished drying the fry pan. We'd had bangers and mash for supper, and scraping the fry pan had been a real challenge.

"So you know who he is."

"He scored three hundred and nine against Pakistan in 2004—one of the greatest performances these eyes have ever seen."

"You were at the game?"

"I was at the test match, young Master Carter."

"I'm Virender Sehwag on Team India," I said.

"Then you have much to live up to. I believe we will dry the fry pan on the burner later. Perhaps you might turn your attention to the cutlery."

"So why did you come here when you did?"

The Butler looked at me. His hands were still in the dishwater. "You have a certain manner of asking surprising questions at surprising times, young Master Carter," he said.

"Because you knew he wasn't coming back?"

The Butler swished the water around. I think he was looking for something to wash so he wouldn't have to answer.

"It's not a googly," I said. "It's a straight bowl."

"Young Master Carter," he said, "answering that question would necessitate—I find it improbable that I am about to use this word, but others seem to pale—it would necessitate blabbing."

"Blabbing on who?"

"On whom. And answering that question would also necessitate blabbing."

"When did you know my father wasn't coming home?"

The Butler said nothing. He found a couple of knives in the sink and washed them. He handed them to me.

"You know," I said, "you're already a blabber, so you may as well tell me."

"You want me to squeal, then?" The Butler suddenly looked appalled. "Did I just say 'squeal'?"

I nodded.

"Thus living in America."

"It's okay," I said.

"It is most certainly not 'okay.'" The Butler opened the drain and watched the water run out. He rolled down his sleeves and put his jacket on. "Young Master Carter," he said, "Donald Bradman was a magnificent batsman, perhaps the greatest batsman to have ever played. As a bowler, however, he at times bowled short on leg stump, considered by some to be a low and ignominious tactic, as you are aware."

"Yup," I said.

"Even an honorable and good man might sometimes act in a manner far beneath him."

"What does that mean?"

"It means that I have most definitely blabbed enough. Now, I presume there is mathematical homework to which you should attend?"

"So he met someone else."

Nothing from the Butler.

"Someone elses?"

"*Elses* is not a plural."

"A whole other family?"

Nothing from the Butler.

"In stupid Germany?"

The Butler looked back in the sink. He found another knife and rinsed it. He handed it to me to dry, and I did.

"How much does my mother know about them?"

"Your mother is a discerning woman, young Master Carter, as well as a strong and loving one. Whatever she knows is hers to know."

"How could he find another family?"

"How can you bowl short on leg stump?"

"It's not exactly the same thing."

"No. It isn't the same thing," said the Butler.

"So why didn't you tell me before?"

The Butler rinsed out the sink. "Decorum," he said. "And now, I think we're done for tonight."

I hung up the dishtowel. "You can be a pain in the glutes sometimes," I said.

"One of my many skills," said the Butler.

· 19 ·

THE YORKER

A yorker is a difficult ball to bowl. The bowler bowls quite long toward the batsman, hoping for a shallow bounce that will pass beneath the batsman's bat and strike the wicket.

NEWS OF THE CRICKET MATCH had gotten around Longfellow Middle School. You could tell when you walked into the lobby and saw the huge British flag hanging down from the stairwell, right next to a red-and-blue sign—with a lion rampant again—that said RULE BRITANNIA.

Ryan Moore walked behind me as I stood looking at the flag waving in the breeze from all the Longfellow Middle School students swarming in. "You must love this, Tory," he said.

I looked at him.

"Do you ever wonder what it would feel like to actually know what you're talking about?" I said.

"Tory," he said, and walked away.

137

"So the answer is no," I called.

Then Billy Colt came and stared at the flag with me.

"It's going to look pretty stupid the day India wins by a million runs," I said.

"But, Carter, India won't be able to score a million runs, because we'll be knocking down all your wickets."

I looked at Billy. "You live in delusion, my friend."

Billy looked up at the fluttering flag. "I wonder if someone from the monarchy will come watch."

I looked up at the fluttering flag. "Krebs is not going to put up with this."

"You think he has a flag of India lying around?" said Billy.

"You think he doesn't?"

Then a shadow fell across us both.

"Unless you're going to start singing 'God Save the Queen,' you better get to homeroom," said Vice Principal DelBanco.

Billy Colt got to "Send her victorious" before Vice Principal DelBanco told him to cut it out.

We walked together to homeroom.

"Tory," I said.

"Takes one to know one," said Billy Colt.

Mrs. Harknet was about to call attendance when we came in. "Here are our cricket players now," she said. "Which of you is on Team India?"

Billy Colt pointed to me.

"So, Carter, are you responsible?"

"For what?" I asked.

Mrs. Harknet looked at me. "Are you pretending you don't know?"

"Know what?"

She pointed to the window, which the entire homeroom was already looking out. So Billy Colt and I did too.

A huge—and I mean *huge*—flag was flying from the pole in front of the school, and it wasn't the flag of the United States. A green bar at the bottom, white bar in the middle, orangy bar at the top. "Saffron," said Mrs. Harknet. In the middle, a blue wheel with spokes.

"Can you guess the nation it represents?" said Mrs. Harknet.

I didn't have to guess.

The flag of India flew broadly in the fall breeze, slowly unfurling, so big that the wind moved across it like long waves.

"It's a nice flag," I said.

"Do you have the combination?"

"The combination?"

Mrs. Harknet sighed. "The pull cable has a combination lock on it now. We can't take down the flag until we have the combination."

I looked out the window again. Another set of waves unfurled the flag slowly.

Mrs. Harknet sighed again. "You may as well take your seats," she said.

ℯ ℯ ℯ

In Physical Science, Mrs. Wrubell sort of eyed me when I came in. "So are you one of the miscreants?" she said.

I wasn't sure what a miscreant was. "I don't think so," I said.

"I should hope not," said Mrs. Wrubell.

In social studies, Mr. Solaski said, "Are you seriously playing a cricket match?"

Billy Colt and I nodded.

"Cricket?"

Nodded again.

"And that's what the flags are all about?"

Nodded one more time.

"Cricket?"

"The most lovely and sportsmanly game that mankind has yet conceived — or ever will conceive," I said.

Mr. Solaski looked at me.

"Okay," he said.

In Math Skills, Mr. Barkus posed a word problem: "If a large flag flying outside decays by ten percent each year, how many years will go by before the flag is unflyable? We will assume for purposes of this problem that a decay of eighty-five percent equals unflyable. And to avoid embarrassingly simplistic responses, I will tell you that the correct answer is *not* eight years."

Vice Principal DelBanco never did get the flag down. At the end of the day, the buses waited underneath its broad waves, the pride of India waving and unfurling its green and white and saffron bars above us all.

Late that afternoon, it started to rain. I mean, really rain. Like an Australian tropical thunderstorm.

I decided to clean my room.

Sort of.

I took the photograph of Captain Jackson Jonathan Jones standing in front of an American flag and folded it in half. Then I ripped it in half. Then I ripped the halves in half again. Then I put the pieces in the garbage.

I took the beret from his first deployment and balled it up. I tried to rip it in half, but I couldn't. So I put it in the garbage.

Then I took the goggles that still had sand in them from Afghanistan, and I twisted them all together, and after I twisted them all together I stomped on them until the eyepieces were broken and the sand of Afghanistan was sprinkled over the floor. Then I put them in the garbage.

I lay down on my bed.

I listened to the Australian tropical thunderstorm.

When the rains came while we were in the Blue Mountains, my father and I would lie in our tent. I wished I could remember what we talked about. I know I tried to talk about Currier, but he didn't want to talk about Currier, and I almost began to cry whenever I tried, so I never showed him the green marble. Once he tried to tell me about Afghanistan, and Germany, but the rain got too loud and we stopped talking.

Because the rain was too loud.

Before supper, the Butler knocked, opened the door, and looked in.

"You'll be down for dinner in fifteen minutes," he said.

"Yup."

"*Yup* is an Americanism as barbarous as—"

"Yes, I will be down in fifteen minutes, Mr. Bowles-Fitzpatrick," I said.

"Much better," he said.

Then he saw the space on the shelf above my desk.

The Butler looked at me.

I looked at him.

"Did it help?" he said.

"A little," I said.

"Have you talked with your mother about . . ."

"A little. It hurts her . . ."

The Butler nodded. "Only her?"

I didn't say anything.

The Butler stood at the end of the bed. "It will hurt to be angry at him, but you *will* be angry at him."

"I'm not mad at him," I said.

"I suspect that is not true," said the Butler.

"I'm not."

"Young Master Carter, unless you are Mother Teresa in disguise, I would find it extraordinary if you were not angry. There is no shame in—"

"So I'll be down in fifteen minutes," I said.

The Butler nodded, but he went over to the trash can. He took out the balled-up beret.

"In fifteen minutes, then," he said.

"Yup," I said.

The Butler left with Captain Jackson Jones's beret.

I lay on my bed.

And I pressed my feet against the footboard.

And I pressed my hands against the headboard.

And I bounced my head up and down on the pillow.

And I bounced my feet up and down on the mattress.

Because he loved someone else more than he loved us. Someone else in stupid Germany.

Because he went to stupid Germany and he didn't love us.

He was gone.

If that isn't a yorker, I don't know what is.

◦ 20 ◦

BLOCK HOLE

A block hole is a hole in the pitch made by batsmen late in the game. Deep block holes may be exploited by bowlers bowling yorkers, as the batsman is thus called upon to "dig the ball" to defend the wicket.

YOU REMEMBER THAT the problem with holding cricket practices on the football field at Longfellow Middle School on Saturdays in October is that the Longfellow Middle School Minutemen play their football games at ten o'clock on Saturday mornings. This means that we get up earlier on Saturdays than we get up on school days—like, before the sun. And since the Butler believed I should walk Ned around the block before we left for practice, this meant I had to get up *really* early on Saturdays.

"You know," I said on the next to the last Saturday of the month, "Annie can walk Ned too."

"Miss Anne is your younger sister," said the Butler.

"What has that got to do with it?"

"Neither your mother nor your sisters should be walking the dog."

"Because . . ."

"How curious it is, young Master Carter, not only to begin your sentence with a subordinating conjunction, but to trail off vocally as if I were expected to finish the phrase."

"Why can't Annie walk Ned?"

"Your sister cannot walk Ned because she is a young lady."

"Girls can't walk dogs?"

"Not when they have older brothers."

"Mr. Bowles-Fitzpatrick, I think it's illegal to believe that anymore."

"It certainly is. Here is Ned's leash. You should have sufficient time to get him to the dying day lilies before necessity strikes."

That's what Saturday mornings before cricket practices were like with the Butler.

Here's what an afternoon practice the week before the match between Team India and Team Britannia was like:

Krebs batted about a thousand balls out to the Team India slips and made them sprint back in with them.

Then Krebs batted about a thousand balls out to the Team India covers and made them sprint back in with them.

Then Krebs batted about a thousand balls out to the Team India mids and made them sprint back in with them.

And while the slips and covers and mids ran after the thousands of balls, the rest of us took turns as batsmen running between the wickets. "You've got to sprint on the first run to see if you can make more," Krebs hollered. So we sprinted on the first runs until Hettinga started to crawl between the wickets and Krebs took pity on us and made us take turns bowling against him.

"Remember," he said as he was striking every ball we threw, "it's a true wicket. The advantage is all to the batsman." And "You got to keep your foot behind the crease." And "A ball from a pace bowler comes in fast, but it gives fielders less time to get ready. So be ready all the time." And "Arm over your head. Over your head. No, over!" And "Stay ready out in the field. Stay ready! Catches win matches!"

"You know," Hettinga said while Chall bowled and Krebs hit every one out past the covers, "I think Team Britannia is having a lot more fun than we are."

"Field at gully," said Krebs, "and they won't be having a lot more fun when we're holding the trophy."

"Is there a trophy?"

"You know what I mean," said Krebs. "Chall, you're done. You're one of the bowlers. Jones, you try bowling now."

Bowling isn't easy, okay? Bowling is really not easy, especially when the flag of India is slowly unfurling in long waves on the flagpole in front of the school and you feel like you have this international tradition watching. You have to hold the ball right on the seams. Then there's the run-up toward the batsman, which is like sprinting again and again, except in the middle of the sprint you're bringing your arm up, around, and over your head in a way no human being normally does. And with all that going on, you have to pick your spot where you want the ball to bounce. Plus it's no good if you're not aiming right at the wicket. And the delivery has to be fast or you know the batsman is going to bounce it over the boundaries. You know all this, right?

So it isn't easy.

But guess what. That afternoon, I wasn't bad. I took Yang's wicket on the fourth ball. Chall's on the ninth. And Hettinga? I bowled him for a duck. Not a single run. No kidding.

Then Carson Krebs got up.

"C'mon, quickie," he said.

He swung the bat low a couple of times.

I bowled it, pretty long.

He batted it out farther than any Longfellow Minuteman could throw a football.

I bowled it even longer.

Way farther than any Longfellow Minuteman could throw a football.

I bowled it close in.

Way, way farther than any Longfellow Minuteman could throw a football.

"You're not going to get my wicket that way," Krebs said.

I bowled it twice more, fast.

He swung as if he were out for a stroll, and smiled as the balls scooted past the mid-off.

Then I bowled the yorker.

It came off okay.

It spun okay.

It hit a little before Krebs's feet and flew toward his wicket—exactly what it's supposed to do on a true wicket.

Krebs followed it the whole time, and smacked it into the covers.

He smiled at me. "Nice try," he said.

A couple of googlies next, spinning inside.

I think he hit them with only one hand on the bat.

So then I set up for the next bowl. I felt around the ball until I could hold the seams just right.

"That's not going to help," said Krebs.

I practiced bringing my arm up over my head.

"Still won't help," said Krebs.

I began the run-up. Krebs gripped his bat straight.

And I eyed the spot for the bounce, and rounded my arm, and bowled the ball about as fast as you can bowl a cricket ball, and I delivered it longer than any I'd delivered before, and this time, straight to Krebs's off stump—no spin, right at his feet.

A yorker.

A real yorker.

Let's just say that when his bails went flying, I sprinted back toward my wicket, slid across the grass on my knees, ripped off my shirt, pumped my arms, and hollered like we'd just won the World Cup of Cricket.

And guess what. That's what all the slips and covers did too.

Every single one.

Hollering with our shirts off, pumping our arms — and it was cold, so this was a big deal.

And Carson Krebs stood at his wicket, holding the bails, leaning on his bat, smiling. "When you guys are all done," he said, "we can get back to work. It looks like we've finally found our other bowler."

After three days of unfurling in long waves, the flag of India was taken down late one night.

Principal Swieteck never investigated. She had her flagpole back, and besides, it wasn't hard to figure out who had taken it down. Or put it up.

But Vice Principal DelBanco still wasn't walking around happy, and I don't think it was because of the flag of India. I think he was getting more than a little annoyed with cricket, mostly because the only thing anyone was talking about was the match between Team Britannia and Team India. At Longfellow Middle School, in the last weeks of October, the only thing anyone was supposed to be talking about was Minutemen football. And no one was talking about Minutemen football.

Like in Mrs. Harknet's homeroom, when Vice Principal DelBanco proclaimed during morning announcements that this Saturday the Minutemen would be playing football against the Seton Badgers.

"So, are you going to bowl the whole time?" asked Patty Trowbridge.

"This will be the fourteenth meeting of these two rivals," said Vice Principal DelBanco over the PA.

"The whole match," I said. "Chall and I bowl every other over."

"Currently, Seton holds an eight to six advantage over the Minutemen," said Vice Principal DelBanco.

"Over?" said Patty Trowbridge, like a stupid sixth grader.

"Six balls," I said.

"But this year, our offense has averaged twenty-four points per game," said Vice Principal DelBanco.

"What position is Krebs batting?" said Jennifer Washburn.

"The second highest in our conference," said Vice Principal DelBanco.

"He hasn't decided, but probably third," I said.

"And we have every confidence that the Minutemen will score big against their archrivals."

"If he's the best player, shouldn't he be batting fourth?" said Mrs. Harknet.

"So come out to cheer your team on. Ten o'clock for the kickoff!"

"Number three is the most important," I said. "By fourth, the bowlers are getting tired, and the third is the guy responsible for tiring them out."

"So who's up first?" said Jennifer Washburn.

"Come support your team!"

"Krebs hasn't told us who the opening batsmen are. Maybe Chall at number one, Briggs at number two."

"Bring your family!"

"This Saturday?" said Mrs. Harknet.

"This Saturday!" said Vice Principal DelBanco. "Ten o'clock. Don't forget!"

"This Saturday," I said. "Eight o'clock."

"Go Minutemen!" said Vice Principal DelBanco.

"I'll be there," said Mrs. Harknet.

She would probably be the only one in the bleachers on Saturday morning at eight o'clock. But still, it's nice to know your homeroom teacher is going to show up.

I guess that's about decorum too.

• 21 •

THE FLY SLIP

The fly slip is a position in the outfield beyond the slip, designed to catch deep hits and so prevent multiple runs.

ON THE WEDNESDAY before the match, the Butler drove me home in the Eggplant after practice. And it had been a pretty hard practice, with me bowling half the time, Chall the other half, and batting and sprinting between wickets and fielding as a slip when I wasn't bowling. I was about as tired as a cricketer on Team India can get, and I wasn't exactly looking forward to walking Ned around the block. So when we pulled in to the driveway and Annie was already on the stoop with Ned on a leash, I figured that maybe there was justice in the world.

But the Butler didn't agree.

"Young Master Carter will escort Ned," said the Butler when we got out.

"I don't mind," said Annie.

I looked at the Butler. "It's okay," I said.

"I can walk him," said Annie.

"She can walk him," I said.

"In general, Miss Anne, young ladies do not—"

Annie put her hands on her hips, and she gave That Look. No kidding. "We're in America, Mr. Bowles-Fitzpatrick."

He looked at her. He looked at me. He looked at her again. "So we are," he said finally. "We shall accompany you."

Which wasn't exactly what I wanted to do.

But we did.

It probably looked kind of ridiculous, three people walking a dachshund past the Ketchums' green and browning azaleas, the Briggses' green and browning rhododendrons, the Rockcastles' green holly hedge with its red berries, and the Koertges' dead petunias, until we got to Billy Colt's driveway and we all waited while Ned pooped, and then we all waited by the day lilies—that were looking sort of yellow now, probably because it was late October—while Ned did what he had to do.

And while Ned was doing what he had to do, Annie looked at me and said, "Daddy isn't coming home, is he?"

I thought I was going to throw up—like a dachshund.

"Did Mom talk to you about it?" I said.

"Is he?" she said.

"You should talk to Mom," I said.

"Young Master Carter," said the Butler—and he said it in

153

a voice like the kind you hear in quiet dreams—"Miss Anne is asking her older brother a question."

I looked at the Butler. "Blabber."

"She is asking her older brother to tell her the truth," he said.

Ned finished with the day lilies.

In the Blue Mountains of Australia, you wouldn't even notice day lilies like the ones at the end of Billy Colt's driveway. All the plants in the Blue Mountains of Australia have these huge leaves, and they're all overlapping, and they're always dripping from the thunderstorms, and they're so thick you can hardly get through them when you try to. They're so thick you mostly can't see the ground.

In the Blue Mountains of Australia, Ned would get lost right away, the moment he stepped off the path. And who knows what kind of snake would be slithering in the low grass, waiting for him? In the Blue Mountains of Australia, the snakes waiting for you if you step off the path are mostly poisonous. If you get bitten, you're not going to make it back to any ranger station. You're just not.

You have to pay attention, because in the Blue Mountains of Australia, there's stuff you can't see. There's stuff you don't even want to see. Or want to talk about.

"Is he?" said Annie.

"No," I said. "He's not."

The Butler took Ned's leash from Annie, and Annie put

her arms around me, and she put her head against my chest, and she cried.

And cried.

We stood there a long time — so long that Ned decided to use the day lilies again.

And when he was about to use them a third time — that's how long we stood there — Annie looked up at me, and she said, "Was it something we did?"

I looked at the Butler.

"Miss Anne wants you to tell her the truth," he said.

I held Annie's head against me, and I said, "Not something you did."

Then we all walked back.

Once home, the Butler told me to get cleaned up, and I stood under the shower that pelted me like an Australian tropical thunderstorm, and when I came downstairs again, Annie and Charlie and Emily and my mother were on the couch together, and they were all crying. I sat next to them — it was sort of crowded — and Emily did something she hadn't done for a long time: she climbed onto my lap and put her arms around my neck and hung on like everything in the whole world depended on it. I didn't think she was ever going to let go. And you know what? I didn't think I was ever going to let go either.

❧ ❧ ❧

That night, my mother suggested pizza for supper, even though the Butler said, "Madam, permit me to protest."

"Let's make it easy this one time," my mother said.

He looked at her. "Pizza is Italian," he said.

"The children all like it," she said.

"Have you ever eaten pizza?" I asked.

"Perhaps you misheard my recent ethnic identification, young Master Carter: pizza is Italian," said the Butler.

"So that's being objective in order to discern and express truth?"

"There are limits to all dicta," said the Butler.

"You can't say you don't like pizza if you've never tried it," I said.

"And yet, there are so many things I *can* say that of— monkey brains, squid tentacles, whale blubber. I feel quite confident in adding pizza to the list of things I know I would detest despite not having tried them. Never mind the fact that one would always do well to avoid food served out of an automobile."

"Can we have pepperoni on it?" said Emily.

"And pineapple?" said Charlie.

My mother looked at the Butler. "One night," she said.

The Butler hesitated, hesitated, hesitated . . .

"And sausage?" said Emily.

The Butler heaved this great sigh of despair, like he'd just heard the whole world was about to end or something.

"In for a penny," he said, and went to make the phone call.

We waited about twenty minutes, and then the Butler said we should all get into the Bentley and drive to Willy's Pizza and Subs, so that at the least, our dinner would not be afflicted by the erratic driving of Willy's proxy.

"What's a *proxy*?" said Annie.

"A teenager," said the Butler. "Step lively now, please."

I drove. My mother sat in the back seat, gripping the three girls with tight hands.

But can I say, besides the one stop sign that was pretty much hidden by a stupid spruce tree that whoever owned should have cut back, I did fine?

The pizza was ready when we got there. Two pepperoni and pineapple and sausage and green pepper pizzas. The green peppers were the Butler's idea. "We may as well have at least one item for dinner that makes an appearance on the food pyramid," he said. So we sat around a table beneath a television—you can imagine what the Butler said about sitting beneath a television—at a table with a plastic table-cloth—you can imagine what the Butler said about the plastic tablecloth—and the Butler served slices to all of us and then he took a piece of pizza onto his own paper plate—you can imagine what the Butler said about the paper plate—and he asked for a proper fork and knife and Willy himself brought a plastic fork and knife—you can imagine

157

what the Butler said about the plastic fork and knife—and the Butler ordered a ginger ale because they don't serve tea at Willy's Pizza and Subs—you can imagine what the Butler said about Willy's Pizza and Subs not serving tea—and we picked up the pepperoni and pineapple and sausage and green pepper slices—you can imagine what the Butler wanted to say about us picking up our food but didn't—and we ate all of it.

Willy asked the Butler how he'd liked his pizza when he had finished.

"It abounded in mozzarella," said the Butler.

"That's what we're known for: extra cheese," said Willy.

"And the proximate nature of the green peppers and the pineapple was remarkable," said the Butler.

"I arranged it myself," said Willy.

"And the pepperoni and sausage were as pungent as any human being might wish."

"Only the best ingredients," said Willy. "So you liked it?"

"The night will go down in the annals of digestive history," said the Butler, and Willy slapped him on the back.

"Next time you come, you'll try the Willy Supremo."

"The very next time," said the Butler.

• 22 •

RUN OUT

If a batsman attempting a run cannot reach the crease before the ball is thrown into it, and the bails are knocked off, then the batsman is out. Any fielder may knock down the bails, and so the batsman is out. When a batsman is run out, his turn is over.

IT WAS a hard night.

The girls kept waking up, and they would remember, and then they would start to cry, and I would listen to my mother walking down the hall to their bedrooms. The sounds of quiet voices in the dark, soft and sad. Charlie and Emily whispering after my mother left. Annie in their room. And then finally all three of them in my room, carrying blankets and pillows and Ned and climbing up on my bed and all of us lying down together in some sort of tangle. (This is not something to tell Billy Colt, remember.) Finally falling asleep with someone on top of me, or maybe two someones on top of me, or maybe two someones and a dog on top of me. Waking up a couple of times with lots of breathing in the room, and being happy about all that breathing.

Really happy about all that breathing.

Even Ned's.

But it was still a hard night.

So when we bundled into the Eggplant the next morning, we were pretty sleepy. And it was raining, of course, not as hard as an Australian tropical thunderstorm, but the wipers were swishing back and forth fast, and the Butler had to lean forward to peer through the windshield.

We stopped first at St. Michael's to drop off my mother, who was, if you can believe it, leading a meeting to plan the budget not for next year, but for the year after next year! I guess there really is no time to lose.

After that we drove to Longfellow Elementary, and when we arrived at the second-grade door, the Butler got out with his satellite-disk umbrella, opened the side door, leaned down, and said, "Miss Emily, make good decisions and remember who you are."

"Are you going to be here after school?" said Emily.

"Of course I will be here," said the Butler, and she hugged him under the umbrella.

When we got to the fourth-grade door, the Butler got out with his satellite-disk umbrella, opened the side door, leaned down, and said, "Miss Charlotte, make good decisions and remember who you are."

She hugged him under the umbrella.

When we got to the fifth-grade door, the Butler got out with his satellite-disk umbrella, leaned down, and said, "Miss Anne, make good decisions and remember who you are."

She hugged him too.

When we got to the middle school building, the Butler started to get out with the satellite-disk umbrella, and I said, "Don't even think it."

"Of course not," said the Butler. "Why should I deny you the pleasure of sitting in wet trousers and sopping socks all day long by offering the use of my umbrella?"

"Jeans," I said. "Not trousers. Jeans."

"Wet, nonetheless."

I opened the door. "I'm not going to hug you either, you know," I said.

"Have a good day, young Master Carter," said the Butler. "Make good decisions and remember who loves you."

I looked at him. "I thought it was 'remember who you are.'"

The Butler looked back at me. "It is the very same thing," he said.

"What?"

"Young Master Carter, when you walk Ned for your mother; when you attend Miss Anne's robotics competition without observing that such attendance is, if you'll pardon the expression, 'a pain in the glutes'; when you cheer at Miss Charlotte's football match even though she barely had a touch; when you accompany your sister to a Turner art exhibition;

when you take your young sisters to buy Dreamsicles; when you appear as exhibit A for Miss Emily's Favorite Person of the Week event; when you attend two ballet exhibitions despite your unfortunate and undiscerning distaste for the art; you are telling them that it is the same thing."

"Is that sort of what being a gentleman is supposed to be?"

"We are what we love, young Master Carter."

I thought I was going to bawl, like I was still a kid.

I really thought I was going to bawl.

"Mr. Bowles-Fitzpatrick, I—"

"You are letting the rain spatter the upholstery," said the Butler.

"Are you going to be here—"

"As I've already informed your sister, I will be here as usual," he said.

"That's not what I was going to ask."

"Which I am aware of. In you go, young Master Carter."

"You can be such a pain in the glutes," I said.

"Which I am also aware of. It is, as I pointed out earlier, one of my skills," the Butler said.

I ran inside.

But I got rained on pretty hard. The rest of the day, I sat in wet jeans and sopping socks. Somehow, I kept thinking this was the Butler's fault.

And somehow, all day long, I kept remembering who loved me.

◦ ◦ ◦

In the Blue Mountains of Australia, you have to pay attention, you know. If you don't pay attention, anything could happen. Even going to get firewood can be dangerous, because of all the slithering snakes.

But if you never go to the Blue Mountains of Australia, maybe you'd never learn to pay attention.

On the Friday before the match, while I was still remembering who loved me, the school was going kind of crazy—especially in the eighth-grade hallway, where all the lockers had Team India or Team Britannia flags taped onto them.

Every single one of the eighth-grade teachers was wearing a white sweater—and so were some of the sixth-grade teachers, like Mrs. Harknet and Mrs. Wrubell and Mr. Solaski and Mr. Barkus. Mrs. Harknet decided that for reading that day, she would show a film clip. It was so old it was in black-and-white, but it had a Latin teacher playing cricket, and he was really, really good. (I know. This is hard to believe.) Mrs. Wrubell—who wore her white sweater under her lab coat—decided to take a day off from beakers and Bunsen burners to talk about the aerodynamics of cricket balls and why a ball swerves, and she drew a googly on the board and showed how you could predict the way it would move in the air. (I told Billy Colt it wouldn't help him at all.) Mr. Solaski, who was walking around carrying a cricket bat, swinging it wrong because he didn't keep his arm straight, decided to talk about the spread of an empire through examining the game of cricket in Australia, India, and Pakistan. And Mr. Barkus had every single word problem begin with "Two cricketers took their places at the wickets."

At lunch, there were two lines. You could choose either fish and chips or butter chicken with curried rice. You can guess which line Team Britannia went to and which one Team India went to.

And in seventh period, when the whole school was released to the gym for the pep rally to pep up the Minutemen for their big Saturday football game against the Seton Badgers, one side of the gym started to chant "Bri-tan-nia" and the other started to chant "In-di-a" right after the Minutemen were introduced, and the Minutemen looked around sort of confused. Coach Krosoczka thought it was hilarious. Vice Principal DelBanco looked kind of mad, but there was nothing he could do, as Longfellow Middle School got pepped up for the first cricket match in its long and glorious history.

At the beginning of our last afternoon practice, the Butler reminded us that we had to be on the pitch by seven thirty sharp the next morning. "We have only two hours," he said, "and though it is barbarous to shorten a cricket match, it is the case that the Longfellow Minutemen imagine the field belonging more to them than to us, with perhaps some justification, given the peculiar priorities in sport your country has taken. So, seven thirty in the morning without fail."

"Which side are you rooting for?"

"Young Master Krebs," said the Butler, "I do not 'root.' Pigs root. Hogs root. There are undoubtedly other porcine creatures that root. If, however, I were inclined to cheer — please note the correct verb, young Master Krebs — I would suppress the urge in favor of objectivity."

"Does that mean you're rooting for Team Britannia?" said Singh.

"In all matters save the present one," said the Butler. "Now, shall we get to it?"

And we did. I bowled and bowled and bowled, and everyone batted, and the Butler hit to Team India's slip and gully and cover and mid-off on the off side, and the mid-on and midwicket on the on side, and then we switched teams and the Butler hit to Team Britannia's slip and gully and cover and mid-off and mid-on and midwicket, and I bowled and bowled and bowled until my arm was about to fall off and my spinning finger was red and a little bit raw.

"Young Master Krebs, young Master Singh, marked improvement in both teams. I predict a credible match tomorrow morning, which, though low scoring, will be hard fought, and since there have been more than a few well-known test matches of that description — one recalls the 1999 Cricket World Cup semifinal between Australia and South Africa, for example — we shall do the game proud."

"And you're rooting for Team Britannia, right?" said Singh.

"Imagine what you wish," said the Butler.

◔ ◔ ◔

By the time we got the equipment put away and we drove home in the Eggplant, it was already starting to get dark. Cold air was rising up, and the branches—mostly bare now—clacked against one another in a new wind.

"It may be that conditions will not be the best tomorrow," said the Butler.

I looked out the window.

"But your first cricket match, young Master Carter. How splendid for you."

And I guess I should have been pretty excited. I mean, how many sixth graders play on eighth-grade teams By Invitation Only? And how many get to be bowler? So I should have been pretty excited.

"We will need to attend to your finger," said the Butler.

Except I was remembering how the first time I saw the blue air, my father said we should come back to Sydney again someday with all of us and right away I thought, *We can never do that because Currier won't be with us.*

But I hadn't thought, *We can never do that because my father won't be with us.*

Stupid.

"Young Master Carter?"

Stupid.

"Some ointment and a plaster?"

Stupid.

• 23 •

STANCE

The stance is the position the batsman takes when the bowler is about to deliver the ball. A batsmen presents his left or right sides' shoulder pointing down the wicket.

WE DIDN'T EXPECT what happened when we got to the Longfellow Middle School football field on Saturday morning.

We got there in plenty of time. The Butler made us all get up early—my mother and Annie and Charlie and Emily too. Ned was pretty excited, I guess because he knew something unusual was happening, so he threw up twice. I walked him around the block while the Butler cooked Irish steel-cut oatmeal. "One need not deplore everything that comes out of a nation, despite its lamentable politics," he said.

"Unless it's Italy?" I said.

"Lamentably, pizza does overwhelm what might otherwise be attractive," said the Butler.

Emily said she hated oatmeal when the Butler put the

167

bowl down in front of her, and she didn't like brown sugar, and she didn't like raisins, and cream was yucky, and why didn't we ever have one percent milk anymore?

I told you, it was really early.

"It is liable to be blustery on the pitch this morning," the Butler said.

"Cricket is boring," said Emily.

The Butler handed her a spoon. "Miss Emily," he said, "only a dullard would believe such a thing."

"What's a *dullard*?"

The Butler added some brown sugar to Emily's oatmeal. "Currently, your television stations are spending most of their time airing three-hour-long orgies of what Americans mistakenly call football. If you were to watch the commercials—and you shall not, lest you be infected—but if you were to watch them, there would be no need to ask such a question. Now, to the task at hand, please."

"Emily," I said, "if you eat your oatmeal, I'll let you bowl the first ball."

"Really?" she said.

"But you have to eat all your oatmeal."

"The first ball?"

I nodded.

Emily was the first one finished with her Irish steel-cut oatmeal, and after we all finished too, we piled into the Eggplant, the girls wearing coats, since the Butler had been right and conditions were not the best. I wasn't wearing a coat. I had on my white sweater—which was still too long, but I was used to it. "You will need the freedom of your arms today, young Master Carter," said the Butler.

"Suppose I get cold?"

"Then you shall bowl all the more vigorously," said the Butler.

And so we came to the Longfellow Middle School football field, at seven thirty in the morning, and we parked the Eggplant in the school parking lot. Krebs was already there, and his father too. And Coach Krosoczka. And in just another minute or so, everyone from Team India and Team Britannia was there as well, jumping up and down, and beating and holding our arms around ourselves because it really was cold and windy—"blustery," said the Butler.

"Freezing our glutes off," I said.

"I think it might snow," said Coach Krosoczka.

The Butler took some blankets out of the trunk for my mother and sisters, and he handed me three bright red new cricket balls and three new bats—"Mr. Krebs senior and I have knocked them in ourselves," said the Butler—and we headed toward the Longfellow Middle School football field, the home of the Minutemen.

And that's where the thing we never expected to happen happened.

"What's that sound?" said Emily.

"The wind," said Annie.

But it wasn't the wind.

169

It was the crowd.

Mrs. Harknet wasn't the only one from Longfellow Middle School there after all.

The stands were full.

That's right. Full.

Full!

I know. I couldn't believe it either.

"What are all these people doing here?" I said.

"Soon there will be a cricket match played on this field," said the Butler. "Where else would they be?"

"Asleep?" I said. "Or watching *Ace Robotroid and the Robotroid Rangers*? Or raking leaves? Or . . ."

"Young Master Carter," said the Butler, "there is time enough for all that. Now is the season for cricket."

"*Ace Robotroid* comes on only on Saturday mornings."

"And no one here seems to care about that in the least," said the Butler, and he waved his hand toward the stands.

"I guess they're not dullards," said Emily.

The Butler leaned down. "You, my dear, are exactly right. Now, here's the ball. Let me show you where to stand, and your brother will bat." Which I did, four times because Emily said the first three didn't count because they only rolled to me. I took a few steps toward her and the fourth one did reach me and I batted it out to Krebs, and he threw the ball back in, and then he bowed to Emily—really, he bowed—and Emily was so happy she would have thrown up if she were a dachshund. Then I took her hand and walked her over to my mother in the stands, where everyone was cheering for her.

And the stands were really, really full.

I leaned down to her. "Was it worth the oatmeal?"

She nodded.

I could see Mrs. Harknet, and Mrs. Wrubell, and Mr. Solaski, and Mr. Barkus. Principal Swieteck was there in her white sweater. I think most of the sixth grade was there, and probably most of the eighth grade, and even some of the seventh grade. But there were lots of other people too, and I don't think they were there just to get a good seat for the Minutemen game. There were a lot of parents and grandparents and little kids. One kid was leaning over the rail, holding up both his arms and cheering like he wanted to be out on the field with us. Two old guys were all decked out in white sweaters—probably cricketers once. And Billy Colt's parents were there, and a bunch of girls Annie knew from fifth grade, and Sarah Bixby—who was cheering like a wild child—and Patty Trowbridge, who waved at me, and Jennifer Washburn, who waved at Krebs but he didn't notice, and even—if you can believe it—a news crew from WZZN stringing long cables and fussing around with two cameras.

"Is this on television?" I said.

"Depends on whether it's a busy news day," said the cameraman.

I told the Butler, who was putting on a white brimmed hat to go with his white shirt—he must have been freezing his glutes off—that the match was going to be on television. He looked over to the cameras. "Perhaps Ace Robotroid himself will be preempted," he said.

"Don't count on it," I said, and the Butler handed me the stumps.

"Young Master William is just arriving. Shall I leave it to the two of you to put the stumps out? On the thirty-nine-yard lines, please. We may as well play dead center."

So I took the stumps and I handed the bails to Billy Colt, and we went out to the thirty-nine-yard lines and started to pound the stumps in, and the whole crowd got really quiet—either because they were trying to figure out what we were doing or because they were waiting for Vice Principal DelBanco to come out and start to pound *us* into the ground. But when we had the stumps in and the bails set on top, the crowd began to clap as if we'd done something amazing, and Billy Colt took a bow like Krebs, and they all went wild.

"What are you doing?" I said.

"They're cheering for Team Britannia," Billy Colt said.

"No, they're cheering because we pounded in the stumps."

He took another bow. More cheers. "Pretty soon they'll be cheering for Team Britannia," he said.

"Believe it while you can," I said, and we headed back to the Butler, and to the eighth-grade varsity cross-country team, except now they were Team India and Team Britannia. They were all wearing white sweaters, and Krebs was holding a bat and swinging it low, and Singh was lobbing slow bounces to his wicketkeeper, and Team Britannia was warming up with short sprints, and I think we all could feel the eyes in the stands, and the lenses of the cameras, and the cheering of the little kid whose father was holding him now—probably so he wouldn't fall over the railing—and the steady glare of the two old guys in white sweaters, who were standing up and looking like they were ready to captain us if only we'd ask.

They really must have been cricketers.

And that little kid! He looked like he would have given anything right then to be a cricketer. Just like Currier would have given anything right . . .

Just like.

The Butler and Coach Krosoczka waved us in and we gathered around them. The wind was whistling like it does in the Blue Mountains, and I looked up into the stands and wished I had one of the blankets that my mother and Annie and Charlie and Emily were cuddling around themselves.

"I am pleased to see you all wearing your whites," said the Butler, "and that no one has succumbed to the temptation to wear the pajama kits that have become so fashionable."

"Who wears pajamas to play cricket?"

"Barbarians, Master William. Now, to it. Coach Krosoczka and I are the umpires, the ultimate arbiters of the game," said the Butler. "Both whining about and disagreement with any of our decisions is unseemly and discourteous, and so will not occur on this pitch. Are we all agreed? Good, then. It will be my responsibility to oversee the coin toss, to monitor the number of runs, to be sure there is no running short—as, Master Briggs, is sometimes your tendency, so be on your guard, for I will call it mercilessly—to signal when the ball is in, to respond to all appeals, and to mark all breaches of discipline—of which there will be none, gentlemen. Batsmen, you will take your guard in a timely manner, and bowlers, you will deliver without long delay. We play only a single innings, so the game will be abbreviated, given the ten o'clock necessity of the Minutemen. We will have time for six overs to a side, six bowls for each. The fielders are restricted to seven per side. This means, of course, that we will not be playing a true match. Nonetheless, Coach Krosoczka and I expect the full attention and intensity of such a match from both teams."

We nodded our heads and huddled closer—mostly to hide from the wind.

"We begin with the coin toss." The Butler handed a coin to Singh.

"What's this?" he said.

"It is a pound," said the Butler. "If you would be so kind, please toss it and spin it in the air, calling heads or tails. Whoever wins the coin toss will bat first."

"How will I know which is which?"

"The regal profile of the queen will be a clue."

So Singh tossed the coin and called, "Tails!" and we all looked in to see it fall, and the Butler called, "Tails it is!" and Team Britannia cheered and Hopewell and Bryan ran to their wickets, and Krebs positioned the fielders—Steve Yang was wicketkeeper—and then he handed the ball to me, and he said, he really said, "Remember, this is cricket. So pay attention."

And suddenly, the wind sneaked between the stands of the Longfellow Middle School football field and coiled around the thirty-nine-yard lines. It hunted and slithered and scrambled around us, then bit deep—like our white sweaters were its target, and it meant to freeze our glutes off.

It was the kind of cold, wet wind that comes just before an Australian tropical thunderstorm blows in.

I looked over at the stands. The little kid's father had wrapped a blanket around him, and the little kid was still cheering, and his father was cheering with him and holding him tight.

And that's when I felt the Blue Mountains of Australia lean over me.

Like I had always known they someday would.

• 24 •

SLEDGING

Sledging is the act of a fielder — sometimes with good nature, sometimes with aggression — who seeks to distract the batsman through taunts and heckles as the batsman tries to concentrate.

I WAS THERE.

In the Blue Mountains of Australia.

I was wet and cold and the wind was up, and my father had scattered my fire and now he was kneeling by the fire he had built and he was stacking twigs onto it. You could already feel the warmth. Then he was putting on bigger branches and the twigs were crackling and my father held out his hands to the flames.

"You see?" he said.

"I guess," I said.

"You guess?"

A long quiet. Shrieks from the white birds.

"Currier would have loved this," I said.

Currier would have loved this. He would have loved the fire, the trees, the tent, the blue air, the birds—he would have loved everything.

"Max too," he said, leaning another branch into the flames.

I looked at him. "Max?"

"Currier," he said. "I meant Currier."

He reached for another branch.

"Who's Max?"

"A kid I met off base. I took him camping once or twice with his mother. You're right. Currier would have loved this."

"Okay," I said.

"In a little while, it will be time to gather some more wood," he said.

"Young Master Carter, it's time."

I was shivering hard.

Because I was mad.

Because Currier was . . .

Because my father was . . .

Because everything in me was about to come out and I couldn't stop it.

"Young Master Carter, the wicket is yours."

I could feel the green marble hard in my pocket.

Currier's marble.

Currier, who was dead.

I fingered the cricket ball.

"Warming up is in general a—"

"I know," I said. "Okay? I know."

The Butler took a couple of steps back. "Your wicket-keeper is ready," he said.

"I know," I said.

The first warm-up to Yang didn't even bounce before it got to him. In case you've forgotten the rules, that's not a good thing.

The second hit the ground by his ankles.

Yang looked at me, sort of confused.

The third bounced twice and dribbled in.

Yang looked at me, really confused.

Krebs ran in. "You do remember how to do this, right?"

"I remember how to do this," I said.

"So you're just kidding around with those deliveries, right?"

"Yeah," I said.

"Because Chall can always bowl first."

"I can do it."

"Good," he said. "So let's see some bowling."

The next ball bounced just where I wanted it to bounce and it sprang up into Yang's hands like it meant business.

The next one would have taken the bails off.

And the next one.

"Good," said Krebs, "because you don't want to screw up now." And he went out to talk to the slips.

I could hardly breathe.

The screeching of the high birds.

I stood on the wicket. I held the ball.

The little kid in the stands, cheering.

His father holding him.

His father wrapping a blanket around him.

His father laughing and cheering and holding the blanket tight around the little kid.

"Time," said the Butler.

Currier would never see the Blue Mountains of Australia.

"It's time, young Master Carter."

Maybe Max would—but never Currier.

The ball almost fell out of my hand.

In the Blue Mountains of Australia, the air is blue, and everywhere you can hear the water falling, and the trees are so thick you can't see the sky, and you can't go off the path because there are dinosaurs hunting, and poisonous snakes slithering everywhere in the low grass, crocodiles—maybe huge crocodiles—scrambling through the underbrush, and it's stupid to try to start a fire with wood that's wet.

"So is that why you didn't get home before Currier? You were camping with Max and his mother?"

"Don't be stupid, Carter. I tried to get home."

"But you didn't."

"Pay attention to the fire."

And I screamed, "When do *you* pay attention? When *do* you?" And Captain Jackson Jonathan Jones looked at me, and I said, "Never. Never. You weren't home. You never come home. You didn't even come home when Currier was sick.

You didn't come home until he was dead. Until he was freaking dead!"

"Shut your mouth," Captain Jackson Jonathan Jones said.

"So who's Max?"

"A kid. Just a kid. And see? Look at the fire. You screwed it up."

"You screwed up!" I think I screeched that. *"You screwed up!"*

And Captain Jackson Jonathan Jones kicked the fiery branches into the wet grass and water spilled from the thick leaves above them and the white birds screeched at the smell of the smoke. "Get a dry shirt on," he said.

"You didn't come home."

"It's not my fault Currier died."

"I hope you never come home."

"We're leaving," he said.

"Young Master Carter!"

He goes into the tent, and I stand outside, breathing as hard as a human being can breathe, and that's when the snake slithers out of the low grass, winding in curves across the clearing, his flat head so low, his body so long and perfect, the end of his tail swaying, and when he hears my father rustling in the tent, his whole body pauses.

He stops.

He stops right where my father will come out.

Right where my father will step.

And then the Butler was in front of me, and his face was

next to mine, and his hands were on my shoulders, and he looked at me.

Then I see my father's hand at the tent flap.

I don't say anything. Oh, I don't say anything.

My father's head comes out.

The flat head of the snake rises.

My father's knee, and then his foot.

And I don't say anything. Because he isn't paying attention. And we won't make it to any ranger station. We just won't.

Then I scream. I think I scream.

"So it has come to you at last," whispered the Butler.

A shot. All the screeching birds rise up, and the echoes of the shot come back, and back, and back.

And my father looks at me with this look that is surprised and shocked and scared and is filled with anger and—

"Carter," said the Butler.

"When were you going to tell me?" Captain Jackson Jonathan Jones says.

And I'm not sure that I had been going to tell him—and he sees that.

The Butler put his hand on the side of my face.

And I said, "My father isn't coming home because I didn't—"

"No. You had nothing to do with it."

I looked at the Butler. "How could you know?"

"He blabbed."

181

"He blabbed?"

The Butler nodded. "He told me what happened."

Things got kind of blurry.

"I almost let him get bitten by a snake."

"But you didn't."

"But I—"

"Carter," said the Butler, "you did not screw up. Your father did. He did not come when he should have—a pattern, I'm afraid. And he could not face what he had done, and what he was doing, and so he looked for reasons where there were none. In such circumstances, men will do, shall we say, ungentlemanly things."

"Do you know what I said to him?"

The Butler nodded.

"That I never wanted him to come home."

"Which is not true," said the Butler.

"I was mad at him."

"Angry. And that is true."

Blurry.

"But because of me—"

"Stop that. What happened is his dishonor, not yours. Do not heft onto your shoulders burdens you do not own. You are a good and honorable young man, and a loyal and true brother and son."

He paused.

"And a gentleman," the Butler said.

"A gentleman?"

182

The Butler stood straight. "Young Master Carter, I am a gentleman's gentleman. I am honored to serve only a gentleman."

More blurry.

"I'm not crying, you know."

"Of course not."

"Hey," called Singh. "We going to play?"

"Are we going to play?" said the Butler to me.

The echoes of the shot were dying away.

I nodded.

The Butler nodded as well. "We are all in our whites, so we may as well have a go at it," he said. He tightened his hands on my shoulders, and then he let go, and turned, and called out to the eighth-grade varsity cricket team. "Captain Singh, have your first batsman take his guard. Master Hopewell, are you ready? And Master Bryan? So, cricketers, with both batsmen ready, and the bowler properly warmed, it is time. Team India, mind your positions. And Bowler—"

I looked at the Butler.

"Bowler, let us make a good beginning."

You know what? The Blue Mountains of Australia are horrible.

They're horrible.

Everything is wet. The leaves, the path, the air. Everything. The only thing the trees do is drip. Your tent gets wet and smells like it. Your sleeping bag gets wet and smells like it.

You can't go off the path because you might die because of the dinosaurs or snakes or crocodiles, and that's all you're thinking about. And when you're trying to go to the bathroom behind a tree—where the dinosaurs or snakes or crocodiles are waiting—you realize that there's a whole lot of you that's sort of exposed and you don't want to get bitten there. And it's so hot but nothing dries out because it's like being under the ocean, it's so humid. And whoever you're with is crabby and blames you for everything and even blames you for stuff you had nothing to do with and . . . the Blue Mountains of Australia are horrible.

"Let's see that ball," said Hopewell.

Horrible.

"Shall we oblige?" said the Butler.

And I did.

· 25 ·

BATSMEN

Two batsmen always go in to bat together, and they are called the striker and the non-striker. To score a run after a ball has been struck, they must each sprint the length of the pitch and touch the ground of the popping crease. The success of their team depends upon the interdependency of the two batsmen.

OKAY, SO THIS wasn't a match for the ages.

James Hopewell was on twelve—*twelve*—before Krebs, who was at mid-off, caught his shot. "Good ball, bowler," Krebs called back, even though I was lucky Hopewell hadn't hit it out past all the fielders and gone for another six.

Then I gave the ball to Chall and Bryan took his turn to bat and he had scored ten before Steve Yang stumped him. I think you can probably imagine what we did. And then Krebs had Team India run in and gather around their next bowler—me, I mean—and he said, "Okay, we've got things under control now. Stay focused. Okay? Stay focused. And Jones?"

I looked at him.

"Jones, you're doing great. Keep on, okay? Okay?"

185

"Okay," I said.

"How's that spinning finger?"

"Fine."

They went back to their positions and Steve Yang handed me the ball. "Bowl him out," he said.

And Simon Singh stepped up for Team Britannia.

You ever hear of Shane Warne? He was from Australia — I bet he hated the Blue Mountains too — and he once bowled this ball to Mike Gatting, a batsman who could hit just about anything. The ball was way outside leg stump, and Gatting knew it wasn't going to come close to his wicket. In fact, it was so far outside, he decided he'd just block it with his bat and pad. He figured the wicketkeeper would get it and throw it back.

But Shane Warne — who for sure hated the Blue Mountains — bowled with this wicked spin, and when the ball hit the ground, it took off straight for the wicket — beyond Gatting's pad, beyond his bat, even. So when Gatting looked behind him, he saw the bails down, and he was bowled out before he had swung his bat.

I know Shane Warne thought the Blue Mountains of Australia were horrible.

So guess what happened to Simon Singh.

Not that I'm Shane Warne, and not that it was anything more than sheer stupid luck.

And not that it had anything to do with how I was holding the green marble just before I bowled.

Even though maybe it did.

But when Singh looked behind him, his bails were on the ground.

And suddenly the whole of Team India was cheering and cheering and cheering. And that little kid, he was standing up and hollering too. And the two old guys in white sweaters were calling, "Good ball! Good ball!" And then everyone in the stands was standing up, even though I'm not sure they really knew what had just happened, but they were yelling too. And even Simon Singh was nodding his head and smiling. "Good ball, Jones," he called.

The rest of our bowling wasn't as good, but you only get one ball like that in a lifetime, the Butler said later.

Jenkins went for eight before the Butler called him out for hitting the ball twice.

With Klatt I tried a googly and he hit it a long mile. Then I tried another one, since I figured he wouldn't expect it, and he hit it another long mile. So after that I kept the balls low and fast, but he still managed ten before the ball slipped under his bat and he was stumped—and it might have been a little bit because of the blood that my spinning finger was leaving on the ball, but I didn't care.

Chall bowled the final over, and you could tell he wanted to bowl de la Pena for a duck, but you could also tell de la Pena was not going to let himself be bowled for a duck. Still, he only got six runs and then it was the last ball, and the Butler called de la Pena leg before wicket, even though he said he wasn't, and Krebs asked the Butler to let it go, but the Butler gave him That Look and de la Pena left the crease, and Team Britannia had no balls left.

But Team Britannia had scored forty-six runs, and it was already fifteen minutes after nine o'clock.

"Three minutes," called the Butler, and he looked at his watch.

Did you catch that it was already fifteen minutes after nine o'clock? Actually, it was sixteen minutes after nine o'clock. And do you remember that the Longfellow Minutemen were due to play the Seton Badgers at ten o'clock?

And right now the score stood at Team Britannia, forty-six runs. Team India, zero runs. And there was no way we could bat all our six overs in forty-five minutes.

Can you imagine what Team Britannia was doing right then?

Can you imagine what Team India was doing right then?

Can you imagine what Krebs was doing right then?

If you've ever been to a middle school football game, you know that a whole lot is happening in the hour before the game begins—and this was a game where the people in the stands had already been sitting around in the cold for a long time, watching a sport they didn't even know the rules for— except maybe the two old guys in white sweaters. So they were standing and jostling around, probably wondering if the cricket match was over and who won, anyway? Some were tightening the blankets around themselves to keep warm, or getting up to go find Styrofoam cups of coffee, or drinking from silver thermoses that had the Minutemen logo on them. The Minutemen and the Seton Badgers were already sprinting up and down the sidelines, their breath coming out from their helmets like exhaust. They were pounding one another's pads and screaming stuff into the wind and driving their knees up and down like pistons and throwing footballs back and forth, and Ryan Moore and Markie Panetta were bashing into each other, and Vice Principal DelBanco was studying his clipboard and adjusting the headphones that were too big for his head.

In the announcers' box above the stands, two eighth graders were testing the mikes and the speakers—"One two three one two three Go Minutemen one two three"—and I looked over at the Butler, who looked over at me and then looked over at Krebs and then said, "Right." He motioned to Coach Krosoczka and together they sprinted over toward the stands.

Well, kind of sprinted. The Butler was portly, remember.

Meanwhile, Team India and Team Britannia gathered on the wicket. And maybe I was the only one of us who saw what I saw: the Butler and Coach Krosoczka stopped in the stands, called to Mr. Krebs, and then all three went to talk to Principal Swieteck.

The wind was picking up and it was getting a whole lot colder, so we gathered in close.

"I guess we're not going to be able to bowl all our overs," said Singh.

Krebs held a bat. He looked around at the stands, and at the Minutemen, who now were running drills on the field.

"I guess," he said. I thought he was going to cry.

Hopewell—who could be a jerk—grinned. "So Team Britannia wins, right?"

Krebs stared at him. If he had the right superpower, he could have shriveled Hopewell down to a small pile of mucus inside a white sweater.

I stood next to Billy Colt. "Hey, you okay about not batting?"

He looked at me like I was a stupid sixth grader. "Are you kidding?" he said. "It was the best moment of my life." He pointed to the stands. "Do you want to bat in front of everyone? And it's an eighth-grade team anyway."

I nodded. I sort of knew what he meant.

And that was when the two eighth graders in the announcers' box thumped on their mikes again. "One two three one two three. Can you all hear us? Raise your hands if you can hear us. Okay. So we've got an announcement from Principal Swieteck." You could hear the mike being passed over and one of the announcers saying to Principal Swieteck, "You have to get closer. Closer. Okay, you're on. No, you're . . . now. It's live now." And then she came on.

"Good morning, good morning. Is this on? Are you sure? Good morning, parents and grandparents and students and

190

friends and sponsors. This is Principal Lilian Swieteck speaking. Thank you for coming out for this great event—really, two great events: the epic battle between the Longfellow Middle School Minutemen and the Seton Badgers, and the very first middle school cricket match between Team India and Team Britannia, coached by our own Coach Krosoczka and Coach August Paul Bowles-Fitzpatrick—who are now crossing the track in front of you."

Applause from the stands.

"Let me introduce them: Coach Victor Krosoczka. Wave, Victor!"

Coach Krosoczska waved.

"Coach August Paul Bowles-Fitzpatrick."

The Butler did not wave.

"And one more introduction: Mr. Lionel Krebs, who as of yesterday was hired by our school district as the new Director of Athletic Activities. Wave, Lionel!"

Mr. Krebs waved.

"I have one announcement: I am delaying the start of the Minutemen–Badgers game by twenty minutes so that Team India may complete all of its batting."

The Butler stopped and looked up at the announcers' booth. So did the two old guys in the white sweaters.

"I'm so sorry—its *overs*. So that Team India may receive all of its overs. Team India is currently behind by forty-six runs, in case you lost track. If you are here only for the football game, you are invited to the snack bar behind the north side of the stands for free coffee. But I encourage you to see the second half of the cricket match, during which . . ."

We couldn't hear the rest of the announcement because everyone in the stands was cheering.

Team India was going to bat.

And no one in the stands left to go to the snack bar—not even for free coffee.

• 26 •

RUN OUT

If the striker should hit the ball in front of him, he will decide whether he and the non-striker will try for a run. If the ball should be batted behind the striker, then the non-striker will decide. This calls for each to judge the skills and speed of the fielders and the possibility of each reaching the opposing popping crease before the ball is thrown back and the batsman "run out."

THE EIGHTH-GRADE varsity cricket team gathered around the Butler, and I said, "How did you do that?"

He was a little out of breath. Portly.

"Young Master Carter," he breathed, "as I have before observed, one uses one's connections appropriately and judiciously. Now, Team Britannia has the opportunity to complete its overs—assuming that the good Vice Principal DelBanco can be persuaded to hold himself from instructing his players to storm the field of Longfellow Middle School. So can Team India marshal a creditable attempt at making forty-seven runs to win?"

"Nope," said Singh.

The Butler looked at Krebs.

Krebs looked back. "My father is the new A.D.?" he said.

The Butler nodded. "As has just been announced."

"How did you do that?"

"The game is afoot, Master Krebs. Are you prepared to captain?"

"I can't believe you did that," said Krebs.

"Call your side," said the Butler.

Krebs grinned and nodded. "Chall and Hettinga, you're openers," he said. Then for the first time I'd seen him while he was holding a cricket bat, Krebs looked like he was somewhere else, and wherever that somewhere else was, it was a pretty happy place.

But everyone in the stands looked like they were right there. The two old guys in white sweaters were pretty excited. They were leaning halfway over the fence and one of the guys was waving this wooden cane and calling something I couldn't hear. And Emily and Charlie and Annie were pretty excited. They were screaming their heads off. And maybe even my mother was pretty excited. She was standing and clapping with the blanket still around her shoulders.

The little kid was asleep in his father's arms.

But you know the Butler was excited too. He looked like Christmas morning.

"August?" I said.

"A noble name, descending in my family from my grandfather's grandfather."

"It's kind of a stupid name. I mean, it's sort of like being named 'September.'"

"Of course, it is nothing like being named 'September.' It is, however, something like being named after a noble Roman emperor."

"Weren't they all assassinated?"

"Young Master Carter, the historians Will and Ariel Durant have written a wonderful if lengthy set of books — *The Story of Civilization* — that stretches to multiple volumes. They are in your proximate future. Now, shall we play?"

"You didn't tell me Krebs's father was the new A.D."

"The right moment had not appeared."

"So how —"

"There are times, many times, young Master Carter, when we find ourselves in a position of great purpose. It may be that the apt word, spoken at the apt moment, leads to great good in the world — and most often, that is a word of kindness and encouragement. And now, I believe your immediate role is to offer encouragement to Masters Chall and Hettinga, who are batting for your team." He turned to the eighth-grade varsity cricket team. "Team India in," he called. "Team Britannia on the field — with dispatch. Master Krebs, your batsmen require bats. Masters Singh and Jenkins, you're our bowlers, correct?"

Krebs handed Chall his bat, and I ran the other out to Hettinga — you know, Krebs looked like Christmas too — and Singh stood on the wicket, ready to bowl, and Team

Britannia stood out in the field, leaning forward, ready to catch, and the stands were cheering—especially the old guys in their white sweaters—and the cold wind was blowing—you can't believe how good it would have been right then to have a cup of hot tea with milk and sugar—and Vice Principal DelBanco was scowling, and Singh was trying to rough up the ball a little bit until the Butler called that illegal and took that ball out of play, and Coach Krosoczka was standing on the track clapping his hands, and Chall was swinging some practice swings, and we had six overs, thirty-six balls, to score forty-six runs— no, forty-seven runs—and you know what? It was just about perfect.

It was so perfect that when Singh delivered his first ball and Chall swung high—probably because he didn't keep his arm straight—and the ball skipped past him and hit the stumps square and knocked the bails six feet away, I was still okay. Even Krebs was still okay—because, you may remember, his father was the new A.D., and Krebs was looking like Christmas too.

Because not *all* the bails get knocked down.

I looked over at my mother. I wonder if she knew that not all the bails get knocked down.

I looked over at my sisters.

Not all the bails get knocked down.

They don't.

❡ ❡ ❡

But even though he was looking like Christmas, Krebs was still captain of Team India. And you remember that when you're playing cricket, you pay attention. So Krebs stood not far behind the wicket, scribbling on a pad, and I knew what he was figuring out. We needed forty-seven runs and we'd already lost our first batsman.

That is, if all of us got to bat before the Longfellow Minutemen took back their field.

Krebs looked a little less like Christmas.

Hettinga scored eleven off fifteen, and then Briggs scored six off four—until he was caught out. He batted for eighteen minutes, because Jenkins didn't hurry with his bowling.

Minutemen sprinting up and down the sidelines, sort of growling.

Yang came in next, and he struck balls like he'd been born to it. He scored twelve easily off six balls, and might have scored a lot more except he thought a spin was coming inside but it was going outside, and he slapped it off the end of his bat and was caught out.

He batted for fourteen minutes.

Vice Principal DelBanco stalking up and down the sidelines, sort of growling.

Krebs scribbling on his pad. Looking less and less like Christmas.

The Longfellow Minutemen and the Seton Badgers throwing passes along the sidelines.

We had twenty-nine runs.

The Minutemen and Badgers gathering in packs in the end zones.

Eleven balls to score another eighteen runs.

And then Krebs handed the bat to me.

"You're the next batsman," he said.

I looked at him. "I'm a sixth grader," I said.

"Obviously," he said.

I looked at the stands. I looked at Team India, huddling together against the wind and the score.

"Shouldn't it be . . ."

"Pay attention, Carter," said Krebs. "You started this. So pay attention."

The sound of high birds screeching—but you know what? Maybe they weren't screeching. Not anymore. Maybe they were calling to each other. Maybe each one was trying to tell another one where he was.

They were calling.

Dang, they were calling.

And I turned to defend my wicket to the death.

You remember the name on my hoodie?

Virender Sehwag.

You know about Virender Sehwag, right? You know he scored 130 against New Zealand—which would win us the game on the Longfellow Middle School football field. He scored 250 against Sri Lanka, and 319 against South Africa. No kidding: 319. And he did it fast. He got his first century with just sixty balls.

That's the guy whose name was on my hoodie, in case you forgot.

Virender Sehwag.

The crowd in the stands was on their feet.

The two old guys in white sweaters were probably ready to have a stroke.

Annie and Charlie and Emily screaming.

My mother standing with the blanket around her shoulders.

Coach Krosoczka still clapping his hands—probably to keep them warm.

Virender Sehwag.

Me.

• 27 •

THE DRIVE

The drive is a stroke by a batsman who is aiming to attack the ball. Usually this begins by waiting for the ball, then setting the forward foot close to the pitch, well forward.

OKAY, SO IT wasn't the most glorious moment in cricket history. Still, it wasn't so bad, either.

Singh stood with the ball in his hand—not roughing it up, but sort of smiling. I think he could feel vengeance surging in his blood.

He shook his arms, eyeing me.

He shook them again, still smiling.

He took his stance—and quacked.

Yup—he quacked.

But you know what? I was in the Blue Mountains once. I had stood where dinosaurs hunt and snakes slither and crocodiles scramble.

I was not going for a duck.

Singh bowled the first ball, and I struck it wide.

I shouted "No" to Hettinga, and he stayed at his wicket. Hopewell already had fielded the ball, and there was no way we would make a run.

But Hettinga shook his head.

The next ball I blocked wide of my wicket.

The next ball I struck well right back at the bowler, and it might have gone a long way. But Singh tipped it up, and Jenkins almost caught it.

Still no runs—and only eight balls left.

Hettinga shook his head again. He probably didn't think a stupid sixth grader should be batting.

He wasn't looking like Christmas.

Singh was sort of grinning this whole time, and every so often he gave his little quack, even though Krebs told him to cut it out.

Then Singh, still grinning, bowled the next ball, and I have to say, it felt like I was getting my eye in, because it seemed to come at me in slow motion, and I knew exactly how it would bounce, and exactly when I should swing.

And I did swing exactly when I should.

The ball took off toward the covers, and I hollered "Yes" to Hettinga and he took off toward me, and I took off toward him, and when we reached the crease, Hettinga hollered

"Yes" and we took off again, and there I was back at the crease, two runs scored.

Two runs!

And maybe I was a little excited. Because when the next ball was bowled, I watched it come at me in slow motion again, and I knew exactly how it would bounce, and exactly when I should swing.

Except the ball came higher than I expected, and the ball hit the top edge of the bat and flew behind me with not much on it.

"Yes," shouted Hettinga, and he took off toward me.

And I took off toward his wicket like there were hunting dinosaurs and slithering snakes and scrambling crocodiles behind me.

Talk about slow motion. You can't believe how long it takes to run twenty-two yards. It takes about a hundred years, even though when Hettinga ran past, he was screaming "Go go go go!"

And you can't believe how it feels to put your bat down into the popping crease.

And then to turn to look at Singh, expecting run number three.

And then to look at Hettinga, who was standing with his hands clasped on the top of his head.

And then to look at a grinning de la Pena, who was standing beside him with the ball.

And then to look at Krebs, who was kneeling on the ground.

And then to hear the Butler: "Young Master Hettinga is run out. Team India, you are down to your last over."

Krebs stood. He laid his pad on the ground. We all knew the score: sixteen runs needed off six balls. He took the bat from Hettinga. He punched Hettinga lightly on the arm. He swung the bat low—once, twice, three times. He walked up to the crease.

Then he looked at me.

I know. It's just a cricket match on a middle school football field on the last Saturday in October. It's not even a full match. Hardly anyone in the stands even got the rules. The Longfellow Minutemen were ready to storm the field, because they didn't care who lost or who won. Maybe none of it made any difference.

But watching Krebs stand with his bat, looking at me, I saw way, way behind him, a kid gathering wet sticks, then building a fire and getting it going all right, and then having it all swept away into the high wet grass. And I wished Captain Jackson Jonathan Jones hadn't done that.

I wished more than anything he hadn't done that.

"Are you—"

"Don't let the bails come down," I said.

Krebs smiled. He laughed out loud. Then he hollered,

"Pay attention, Carter," and Singh handed Jenkins the ball, and Krebs took two more practice swings, and Jenkins got ready to bowl, and so began our last over.

Krebs didn't screw up.

Krebs paid attention.

And it was so beautiful.

The crowd watched from the stands, the two old guys in white sweaters standing the whole time. Vice Principal DelBanco watched. The Longfellow Minutemen watched. The Seton Badgers watched. The guys from WZZN watched and filmed. You know, even the wind that had been blowing pretty hard—not like an Australian tropical thunderstorm, but pretty hard—even the wind calmed down, like it was watching too.

Mr. Lionel Krebs, our new district athletic director, watched.

Everyone watched Krebs, who that day had the sweetest swing any cricketer could ever want.

Who looked like he could do anything anyone could ever hope to do with a cricket bat.

He hit past de la Pena, who was playing cover.

He hit over Hopewell, who was at mid-off.

He hit over Jenkins at mid-on.

It was so beautiful. Coach Krosoczka stopped clapping his hands and just watched. Sometimes, even Team Britannia applauded. It was that beautiful: his eye on the bounce of the ball, the way he followed it into his bat, his extended arm, the smack of the ball against the bat, the blur of him in his whites, running across the wicket like he was gliding.

And I was gliding too.

He'd hit, and yell "Yes," and I wouldn't even watch the ball. I'd just watch him, and run when he told me to. We passed each other again and again, and I made dang sure I ran fast enough to get to his wicket and then back to my own so he could keep facing the bowler. Only once he slapped it behind him, and you know what? He looked at me and watched, until I hollered "Yes," and we ran and ran. And when the last ball was bowled to him, he took it on the upward bounce and drove it, drove it, drove it and bounced it across the boundary, and the Butler cried, "Well done, Master Krebs—four runs!" and Team India went wild and I think you probably know why. And so were the people in the stands, and the Longfellow Minutemen and the Seton Badgers. And Coach Krosoczka was clapping his hands again. And the new A.D.

And the Butler stood at midfield and watched us, holding his arms around his portly self, and when Vice Principal DelBanco came over to shake hands, he did, and right after that, Team India and Team Britannia ran over to the Butler, and I think we would have raised him on our shoulders except, you know, he was portly. And then the Minutemen and the Badgers were all around us, and at the same time the wind released from its hush, spilled from the low clouds, and piled a chilling cold all over us. But even that didn't matter.

The eighth-grade varsity cricket team picked up Krebs—he was a lot lighter than the Butler—and you know who else they picked up? And they carried us both off the field, and we were laughing and waving our bats around, and when we got to the track we had to walk through the crowd and they were cheering and making cricket jokes even though they didn't know any real ones, and someone gave Krebs a flag and it was the wrong one—a British flag, but he didn't care— and he handed me one corner and held the other and it flew in the cold wind, and Krebs said, "Hey, Carter," and I looked at him, and he said, "We kept the bails up!" and the two eighth-grade announcers from the booth above us asked everyone to clear the track so the football game could begin, and it took a long time but we finally did, and so we came to the end of our match.

With the bails up.

With the bails up.

With the bails up!

And the next day, the Butler was gone.

• 28 •

MILESTONES

For both batsmen and bowlers, milestones should be acknowledged with polite, if subdued, clapping. For bowlers, a milestone might mean a striking of five or more wickets. For the batsman, it might mean fifty runs, or a hundred — or sixteen. Accomplishment of all stripes, in cricket as in life, is worthy of honor.

WHEN MY FATHER and I were in the Blue Mountains, we hiked, him in front, me right behind him—always right behind him. We watched the Australian tropical thunderstorms belly in, we watched the skies clear, we watched the air turn that hazy eucalyptus blue. It was always wet enough and hot enough to kill lesser mortals. And except for the hunting and the slithering and the scrambling and the sounds of water dripping or gushing—and the calling of the high white birds—we heard only each other's voices.

Down in the valley of the Blue Mountains, when my father saw something he wanted me to see, he'd say, "Carter," and he'd point. That's all. Just "Carter." And he'd point to some plant or flower like it meant a whole lot, and usually I

207

didn't even know what I was supposed to look at. But he was saying it like he was saying, "I'm glad you're here with me to see this."

I think that's what he was trying to say.

Even if . . . Well, I think that's what he was trying to say.

The Butler was gone for almost a month. I mean, a couple of fortnights.

The note he left said he had an important decision to make—"the making of which requires consultation."

You know how he talks. And writes, I guess.

He didn't tell us when he was coming back. Or why he was being such a pain in the glutes with his "consultation."

Or if he was coming back.

Like . . . never mind.

So, my mother took over like a premier bowler. She made a roster, and when she bowled, we paid attention.

We took turns cooking. My sisters and I one night, my mother the next. I mostly walked Ned, but sometimes Annie did—depending on her robotics club and piano practice. The Marysville Public Library had an exhibit of Rembrandt etchings, and I took Annie in the Eggplant. She liked Rembrandt better than Turner. Emily and Charlie started ballet lessons with Madame Richelieu—my mother took them there in the Bentley. And she picked me up late at school when Krebs and I began running together—along with his father, who said he needed to get in shape again. Mr. Krebs told me I had the makings of a miler. Krebs thought so too. "Better pay attention to that, too," he said.

Late at night, after Emily and Charlie had gone to bed and our homework was done, Annie and I sat with my mother and we held Ba-Bear and talked about Currier—and we didn't cry all the time.

Then one Saturday afternoon, one of those surprising late November days when it seems as if fall is trying to hold on and the light is a dark yellow, the doorbell rang, and the Butler was standing on our front stoop. My mother and sisters had walked to the library to check out the last E. Nesbit book that Emily and Charlie hadn't read, but I was home with Ned, who got so excited he did what he usually does.

"Where have you been?" I said.

"You and Carson Krebs were splendid together," he said.

"What?"

"Few cricketers learn so quickly the importance of depending upon one another. Even fewer discover the pleasures of such dependency. And fewer still learn that such is the very stuff of what makes us most human. You have made good decisions, young Master Carter, and remembered who you are."

"A gentleman?"

"Indeed. Are the bats and balls still in the Bentley?"

"Yes."

"Would you care to drive?"

I drove to Longfellow Middle School and parked, and the Butler opened the trunk of the Eggplant, and together we pulled out everything we needed. We set up a net and pounded in the stumps and placed the bails.

"Defend your wicket to the death, young Master Carter."

"So where were you?"

The Butler paused, the cricket ball in his hand.

"It's a straight question," I said.

The Butler tossed the cricket ball up and down. "Bamberg," he said.

"Bamberg? That sounds like something in a cartoon."

"Bamberg is where your father is stationed, young Master Carter."

A long pause—but no high screeches.

"You went to see my father?"

"You see what reading Sir Arthur Conan Doyle will do for your powers of deduction."

"What did you tell him?"

"I defined for him the qualities of—how shall I say it?—ungentlemanly behavior, in which others are expected to yield to and suffer from the whims of the male line. Then I told him about his son, and his behavior to his sisters, and his support of his mother, and his nobility in the noblest game of all. And I told him that I would be returning to Marysville to witness a rebirth of gentlemanly virtue."

"He's been a jerk to us."

"I know."

"I mean, really a jerk."

The Butler nodded.

"Anywhere else?"

The Butler paused again.

"And to London."

"Okay," I said. "London's cool."

"As you say," said the Butler.

I swung the bat a couple of times. "He might never come home, I guess."

"He might not," said the Butler.

"And then what do we do?"

"The living of your life is hard work, young Master Carter. If that were to happen, you must actively choose what to do. You may act the gentleman or the barbarian."

"Those are the only two choices?"

"Yes," said the Butler, "the only two. And now, may I?" He held up a cricket ball and I swung my bat low, my arm straight.

In Marysville, New York, in a cold November dusk, the air gets a darker and darker yellow. The dark green of the grass spreads out into shadows. The trees are dark but familiar, and the oaks shake their leaves to remind you that they're holding on to them still, even if the wimpy maples have given up theirs. Above them, the sky is streaked with yellow, and red, and crisp gold, and above that, in the dark, the first stars peek, and everything is still and calm.

Late that afternoon, I batted cricket balls high into the golden sky, one after another, just like Virender Sehwag would have.

I might have scored a century.

And afterward, the Butler drove home, and we did not talk, and we pulled into the driveway, and I got out of the Eggplant, and I said, "My father asked you to come to Bamberg, didn't he?"

The Butler looked at me. "He knew that your grandfather's endowment allowed me to choose."

"So he asked you to stay with him."

"Yes, he did."

"And with Max and his mother."

"Yes."

"But you went to London."

"I did."

"How come?"

"I went to London to settle my affairs there."

Suddenly there were three high squeals—the kind that can make a planet stop spinning. The girls were home from the library, and they had seen the Butler in the driveway, and they were pounding toward us.

But before they reached us, the Butler leaned down to me.

"Young Master Carter," he said, "you are my home."

That night, I cried and cried and cried. For Currier, for

everything he would miss. And for my mother, for everything she had missed. And for my father, for everything he would miss.

For me.

Then I chose.

The email I sent had wonderfully descriptive connotations—even though I was saying goodbye.

29

TOE END

The very tip of the cricket bat, the toe end is made of untreated wood. Its owner should pay attention to its particular needs, as it may deteriorate from dampness.

THE BUTLER SAYS, "Make good decisions and remember who you are."

I am Carter Jonathan Jones. I live in Marysville, New York. I am the son of Carolyn Samantha Jones and Jackson Jonathan Jones. I will always be their son.

I am the brother of Anne Elizabeth Jones, Emily Hope Jones, Currier Bronson Jones, and Charlotte Doyle Jones. I will always be their brother.

Ned is our dachshund.

Mr. August Paul Bowles-Fitzpatrick is our Butler. And more.

I am halfway through sixth grade. I am hoping the second half will be easier than the first half.

Mr. Bowles-Fitzpatrick says I am a gentleman. I am going to try to be.

Right now, I am on a plane. Mr. Bowles-Fitzpatrick is in the seat next to me. He's asleep, which isn't surprising since we've been on this plane for seven hours and we have two more to go and there's only so many movies you can watch in a row.

When the Butler told us that my grandfather's endowment allowed for substantial travel, he asked us where we would like to go for Christmas, and we told him.

So we're flying to Italy together.

In my pocket is Currier's green marble. It is always going to be in my pocket.

In my backpack is Captain Jackson Jonathan Jones's beret. The Butler gave it to me before we left. "You will want to have this," he said.

I did.

Across the aisle are my mother and Annie and Charlie and Emily. They're asleep too. Annie is going to a robotics competition in Rome, and while there she wants to sit through a real Italian opera in a real Italian opera house. "That would be lovely," the Butler told her. I put my finger up to my mouth and pretended to do what Ned does — but I guess I'll go anyway. Charlie wants to see a real Italian ballet. I'm hoping they don't like ballet in Italy. And Emily wants to spend a day on a gondola in Venice and she wants to row by herself. That would be okay.

My mother wants to see the Sistine Chapel. Father Jarrett got her special tickets, and when she picked them up at St. Michael's they had a long talk. A really long talk. When it was done, my mother was the full-time administrator of St. Michael's Church.

Guess where we've been going for mass on Sundays again.

The Butler comes too. He likes the architecture of the church. Its central nave, he said, is a credit to its American architect.

And what do I want to do in Italy?

First, I want pizza every night.

You can imagine what the Butler said about that.

But second, I want to climb high up into the mountains of northern Italy. The Butler is going to climb too, even though he's sort of portly, as you might remember.

It's wintertime, so we won't be able to go to the peaks. But we can climb up paths that lead higher and higher until the woods grow thinner and thinner around us, and then there will only be evergreens. The trees will hold up fat boughs of snow, and the air will get colder and colder, and quieter and quieter, and we'll pass high icicles that drip from open rocks, and the snow will crunch beneath our boots, and the sunlight will glint off the snow and the ice, and it will be so bright that we'll have to wear sunglasses in winter.

High up in the mountains of northern Italy, the air will be blue—maybe not blue like the eucalyptus forests of Australia, which I've seen before, so I know what that blue is like. But blue in a different way. In its own way.

The Butler says there are lots of places where the air is blue in its own way.

I've got my eye in now.

I'm going to find them all.